FRIEND OF
THE DEVIL

BOOKS BY JOSH PACHTER

The Tree of Life: The Complete Mahboob Chaudri Stories
The Misadventures of Ellery Queen
(co-edited with Dale C. Andrews)
The Man Who Read Mysteries: The Short Fiction of
William Brittain
Amsterdam Noir (co-edited with René Appel)
The Misadventures of Nero Wolfe
The Further Misadventures of Ellery Queen
(co-edited with Dale C. Andrews)
The Man Who Solved Mysteries: More Short Fiction by
William Brittain
The Adventures of the Puzzle Club and Other Stories
(co-authored with Ellery Queen)
Dutch Threat

The "Inspired by" Series of Anthologies (as editor)

The Beat of Black Wings: Crime Fiction Inspired by
the Songs of Joni Mitchell
The Great Filling Station Holdup: Crime Fiction Inspired by
the Songs of Jimmy Buffett
Only the Good Die Young: Crime Fiction Inspired by
the Songs of Billy Joel
Monkey Business: Crime Fiction Inspired by
the Films of the Marx Brothers
Paranoia Blues: Crime Fiction Inspired by
the Songs of Paul Simon
Happiness is a Warm Gun: Crime Fiction Inspired by
the Songs of The Beatles
Friend of the Devil: Crime Fiction Inspired
by the Songs of the Grateful Dead

JOSH PACHTER, EDITOR

FRIEND OF THE DEVIL

CRIME FICTION INSPIRED BY THE SONGS OF THE GRATEFUL DEAD

DOWN&OUT
BOOKS

Down & Out Books
3959 Van Dyke Road, Suite 265
Lutz, FL 33558
DownAndOutBooks.com

Cover design by JT Lindroos

ISBN: 1-64396-377-5
ISBN-13: 978-1-64396-377-8

TABLE OF CONTENTS

This one's for the Deadheads.
Keep on truckin'!

INTRODUCTION
Josh Pachter

What a long, strange trip it's been, from late 1964 (when Jerry Garcia, Bob Weir, and Ron McKernan of the acoustic Mother McCree's Uptown Jug Champions decided to go electric and form a band they called the Warlocks) to the following November (when, having added Bill Kreutzmann on drums and Dana Morgan on bass, they changed their name to the Grateful Dead) to August 1995 (when Jerry died of a heart attack) and beyond (through the Other Ones, the Dead, Furthur, the Rhythm Devils, Bob Weir & RatDog, Phil Lesh and Friends, and numerous other configurations and solo projects).

As with my previous "inspired by" anthologies—*The Beat of Black Wings: Crime Fiction Inspired by the Songs of Joni Mitchell* (Untreed Reads, 2020), *The Great Filling Station Holdup: Crime Fiction Inspired by the Songs of Jimmy Buffett* (Down and Out Books, 2021), *Only the Good Die Young: Crime Fiction Inspired by the Songs of Billy Joel* (Untreed Reads, 2021), *Monkey Business: Crime Fiction Inspired by the Films of the Marx Brothers* (Untreed Reads, 2021), *Paranoia Blues: Crime Fiction Inspired by the Songs of Paul Simon* (Down and Out, 2022), and *Happiness Is a Warm Gun: Crime Fiction Inspired by the Songs of the Beatles* (Down and Out, 2023)—readers of crime fiction will find plenty to enjoy in these pages: murders, robberies, kidnappings, a cornucopia of crime in all its permutations and combinations. (And one story that's really *not* a crime story, but that I couldn't resist including...)

1

Meanwhile, I hope Deadheads will also enjoy the book—not just as a collection of crime stories, but as a treasure hunt for the connections between the stories and the songs that inspired them. Most of the stories contain "Easter eggs," buried references that will give the Deadicated reader a smile of recognition upon discovery.

The Dead's discography is extensive, and including a story inspired by a song from *each* of their many albums would have made this volume too thick to be affordable. Instead, I've chosen to focus in on the thirteen studio albums...plus their untitled-but-generally-known-as-*Skull-&-Roses* double live album (since it was their first gold record) and a bonus story from another of their live albums (and in a little while I'll explain which one, and why that one).

One of the things I most enjoy about putting these "inspired by" anthologies together is the opportunity to work with authors I haven't previously had the chance to get to know. This time around, that includes Vinnie Hansen, James L'Etoile, Twist Phelan, and Faye Snowden.

I also get a kick out of soliciting contributions from friends in the crime-fiction community, such as Flemish author Dominique Biebau and Americans Bruce Coffin, James D.F. Hannah, Gin Malliet, Kellie Murphy, Kathryn O'Sullivan and her husband Paul Awad, and Joe Walker.

But the *most* fun for me is bringing people into the fold from outside the community, or who are connected to the world of crime fiction in ways other than as writers. This time around that includes David Avallone and Linda Landrigan, and I'd like to take a moment to tell you a bit about each of them:

David Avallone is the son of legendary crime writer Michael Avallone, creator of private eye Ed Noon and many other memorable characters. Mike was a pretty memorable character himself and a good friend. His son David is a well-established author of comic books, but his take on "The Golden Road (To Unlimited Devotion)" from the very first Dead album is his own very first foray into writing straight crime fiction. I know his dad would be proud of him!

If you're a reader of short crime fiction, you probably know that Linda Landrigan is the editor of *Alfred Hitchcock's Mystery Magazine*. She's bought a number of stories from me over the years, and I decided it was high time I buy one from her and was delighted when she agreed to contribute one for this anthology. Although she's been editing short fiction for decades, "Born Cross-Eyed" is her own first published story. "It wasn't easy," she told me, "but I'm glad I pushed myself to do it—and I think the experience will make me a better editor."

Finally, let me introduce you to Avram Lavinsky. By the time he approached me at the Malice Domestic conference in the spring of 2023, I already had authors assigned to all of the Dead's studio albums. Because Avram actually *knew* Jerry and the other members of the band, though, I was interested in getting him into the book, so I suggested he use as inspiration a song from the show the Dead performed at the Wembley Arena in London on October 30, 1990. Why that particular show? Because I was in the audience that evening as the guest of two of my students at the American College in London, who thought it would be funny to watch their elderly—I was thirty-nine!—professor completely out of his element in a sea of Deadheads. As it turns out, though, I was the only one of the three of us who knew all the songs...

Avram remembers: "On various occasions in the late 1980s, I was fortunate enough to spend time with each of the members of the Grateful Dead, but one gathering stands out. I believe it was in the winter of 1988 that rock impresario Bill Graham invited my Dreamspeak bandmates and me to Christmas dinner with Jerry Garcia, Bob Weir, Mickey Hart, Bill and his sons, my band, and no one else. It was a great time to hang with Garcia, because he'd finished up a rehab stint and was healthy and happy. We discussed holiday history and traditions. I'd made an apple pie, and Garcia had seconds. We drank screwdrivers. We talked music for hours. I was surprised Bobby remembered me from an unfortunate event a couple of years earlier, when my band's van broke down returning from a gig in a torrential downpour, and he took me and my guitar player in and let us spend the night in his hotel suite. Garcia explained that such acts of kindness were not unusual for his rhythm guitar player: 'Yeah, he takes in strays.' The Dead shared many of the endearing qualities of our crime-fiction community. They were genuine. They were intellectual. They were welcoming, even to newcomers struggling to get a foothold in their industry."

And on that note, enough with the introductory chitchat. It's time now to cash in our chips, kick the door in, and enjoy the fifteen stories in *Friend of the Devil*!

Josh Pachter
Midlothian, Virginia
April 30, 2024

Grateful Dead
Released March 1967

"The Golden Road (To Unlimited Devotion)"
"Beat It on Down the Line"
"Good Morning, Little School Girl"
"Cold Rain and Snow"
"Sitting on Top of the World"
"Cream Puff War"
"Morning Dew"
"New, New Minglewood Blues"
"Viola Lee Blues"

"The Golden Road (To Unlimited Devotion)" is by
the Grateful Dead.
"Beat It on Down the Line" is by Jesse Fuller.
"Good Morning, Little School Girl" is by Sonny Boy Williamson.
"Cold Rain and Snow" is by Obray Ramsey.
"Sitting on Top of the World" is by
Lonnie Chatmon and Walter Vinson.
"Cream Puff War" is by Jerry Garcia.
"Morning Dew" is by Bonnie Dobson and Tim Rose.
"New, New Minglewood Blues" and "Viola Lee Blues" are by
Noah Lewis.

THE GOLDEN ROAD
(TO UNLIMITED DEVOTION)
David Avallone

Her name was Dawn, as far as I knew. Later I found out it wasn't: she had picked it, with great intention, for reasons both obvious and known only to herself.

In the summer of 1987, I was on my way to California when my beat-up '71 Chevy Impala convertible blew its engine in some desert nowhere and stranded me. I found a furnished dump and got a job in a furniture factory while a sweaty jackass named Reid worked very slowly on my car. Refurbishing the engine would eat up the humble stake I had saved to start my new life, which meant that, even after Reid the Snail finished, I'd have to stick around until I earned it back.

I spent a couple of months assembling the rails that hold cubicles together. It felt like working in a Dickensian workhouse to put together the cells for other poor suckers in some future workhouse. But the pay was fair, as was Dawn, my supervisor.

Even before I knew it was an alias, her name had a fanciful Ian Fleming feel. I clocked in at six every July and August morning and was greeted by a tall and gorgeous woman who called herself Dawn Summers. She had a sunny smile and an explosion of frizzy blond hair like a supernova. She whistled while she worked, and from her it was somehow sweet, rather than annoying. Her eyes were blue and kind, and as blue as they were, they were kinder than they were blue.

She was thirty-something and fun and charming. I was twenty-two and fresh out of school. I wasn't without some kind of rudimentary charm myself, but I'd never asked out an adult woman and was paralyzed by the prospect. Dawn was flirty, sure, but wasn't she at least a little flirty with everyone? There was something in her eyes when she looked at me that I was desperate to take personally, but should I? My confidence was still very much under construction, a fragile structure in need of more concrete and rebar.

By the first week of August, Reid had finally finished the Impala, and by the second week the sack of cash under my bed had almost hit my "time to move on" goal. On the one hand, I couldn't wait to get back on the road. On the other, there was Dawn, and the way she looked at me, which I was desperate to take personally.

One sun-blasted morning, a truck was late with a shipment of rails, and my section of the line shut down. Me and five other guys stood around the loading dock, killing time. Five other guys and Dawn.

I didn't socialize much at work. Our routine didn't allow for more than a few words with each other in the break room. The other guys had all gone to high school together. They called me "Hollywood," because I'd been dumb enough on Day One to explain where I was going. These guys would live and die within fifteen miles of the hospital they were born in, and my kind of dream—the kind you cross a continent for—seemed like a fantasy to them. At first, "Hollywood" was intended to needle me, but we'd grown on each other just enough that it didn't feel like a tease anymore. Just a nickname.

While we waited for the overdue truck, one of the other workers—a handsome dude whose name was probably John—asked Dawn, "What are you doing Saturday night?"

The rest of the boys made predictable noises of surprise and admiration at John's taking the big swing right there in front of us. That was the kind of boldness I didn't yet possess, and I was envious. Also, cliché or no cliché, my heart literally sank. It was a long time ago, but I can still remember my disappointment. Maybe she'd say yes, maybe she'd say no...but how could I ask her out now that John had made his move? It would seem like he'd given me the idea.

But something happened that was completely outside my life experience. Dawn gave him that big sunny smile and said, "I'm busy Saturday night." She took a dramatic pause, then looked directly at me with a shy conspiratorial grin. "David is taking me out."

I would love to report that I was smooth, but I can't imagine my face was clear of surprise. Lucky for both of us, this wasn't the most observant crowd in the world.

"That's right." I probably blushed. "We have a date. Saturday."

The boys made more sitcom-audience noises. (I say "boys," though they were all older than me, some by a decade. But that seventh-grade bio-class boy energy was still there.) Dawn blushed prettily in return, and my heart shot back from the bottom of my stomach, smashed its way through my brain, and shattered my skull on its way to the bright blue desert sky.

Before the situation became unbearably awkward, the truck showed up, and we returned to making partitions to keep future corporate drones separated and lonely.

At the end of the day, I found Dawn in the parking lot, leaning on her Volkswagen Bug. Waiting for me. For *me*. I went a little lightheaded at the sight of her.

"Surprised?" she said.

"Honestly? Yeah."

"Silly boy. I thought I was obvious."

If I'd had the self-awareness back then that I developed in the years that followed, I could have told her that my peer group had treated me like a homely weirdo for most of my life, and a couple of pretty girlfriends hadn't managed to drown out that childhood chorus. But the guy who could have said all that didn't exist yet.

"I wasn't sure. I figured...I'm just some guy passing through. You wouldn't be interested."

She laughed. "An attractive man who's not going to stick around and complicate my life? Baby boy, you're perfect."

From anyone else, I would have chafed like hell against that "baby boy," but I was new at this, and the prospect of a woman wanting to use me and let me go was startling and wonderful.

"There's a pretty good band Saturday night at Jerome's," she said. "Do you dance, David?"

She had never once called me "Hollywood." Another thing the older, wiser me might have taken note of.

Jerome's was a friendly dive bar in an abandoned mining camp just outside of town. Did I dance? After a fashion. I knew how to hold a woman and swing her around.

"I'll pick you up at eight," I said, and tried not to stammer.

Jerome's was hopping, and the band was surprisingly great. They played an impressive array of cover tunes from a wide spectrum of pop, and I felt a particular pang when they hit Steely Dan's "My Old School." But Annandale was over two thousand miles in my rear-view mirror. They followed it with "Cream Puff War," and maybe I should have listened a little closer to the lyrics, like Bogart dancing with Bergman to "Perfidia" in *Casablanca.* Maybe you never notice those things while the story is in progress.

Freed from the confines of the furniture factory, Dawn was a revelation. Dancing with joyous abandon, eyes shining like diamonds in the neon light, singing along, kicking off her shoes and dancing barefoot on the sawdust. I was careful not to step on her pink-painted toes. I could tell she liked my arms around her, liked the gentle pressure on the lower back that telegraphs the upcoming swing. She was a little taller than me and giggled uncontrollably when I dipped her. I played into that a bit and dipped her almost to the floor. "Don't drop me!" she cried.

Dawn, radiating light and heat, uncontainable, captivated the crowd. Every eye in the place was on her, and that suited me just fine. I'd wondered, on the drive to pick her up, if the locals would resent seeing their resident supernova squired by the itinerant city boy...but she was more intoxicating than anything coming out of Jerome's taps, and her joy obliterated any jealousy that might have lingered in an observer's heart.

And then, during what turned out to be our last dance, she pulled me close and kissed me. If there *were* any jealous eyes watching, I was too delirious to notice. I might have started shaking—I was still young enough for that—but a couple of drinks had taken the edge off my nerves.

"Let's go look at the stars," she whispered in my ear.

And we did.

The Fair Grounds were a couple of miles farther out of town. At night, I couldn't tell what made them "Fair Grounds" and not just a patch of scrubby grass in the desert. The nowhere town didn't put out much in the way of light pollution, and I—who'd grown up in New Jersey suburbs—had never seen so many stars.

The star-gazing part didn't last long. Despite our being grown adults who both had keys to rooms with doors that locked, the back seat of my convertible under the starry sky was where it happened. The supernova consumed me, at first with a flattering impatience, then again with slow-motion intensity.

In between, we talked. I can be embarrassingly chatty in the afterglow, or mid-glow, or whatever you want to call it. I talked about where I was going, about my dreams. It didn't occur to me how that might strike her, but she was as kind as her blue, blue eyes.

I don't remember when we collapsed into unconsciousness.

I woke up entangled in her, in every sense you can imagine. The

11

sun was just beginning to crack the sky and flood the desert plain with golden light. I sat up and watched it rise. I looked down at her, and her eyes were open—and just that much bluer and kinder. She sat up with me and took in the view.

"This is my favorite. My favorite time," she said.

"Dawn's favorite time is dawn," I kidded. "That follows."

She smiled, but her mind had gone somewhere else, and she was still there.

"See the road?" she said. "The golden road?"

I followed her gaze to the lone country lane that ran from horizon to horizon. The daybreak had painted it with molten sunlight.

"It's like the Yellow Brick Road, but even more beautiful, more..."

She trailed off. Thoughtful.

"It's an invitation," I offered. "To go and keep going,"

She turned to me, nodding. "I knew you'd get it. You were following it, following the golden road, when you got ship-wrecked."

I gestured to the Impala's endless black hood. "It took him a while, but Reid has repaired the mast and patched the hull."

I wouldn't say she frowned, but she got serious. I put my arms around her and kissed her. "That doesn't mean I'm going. Not—"

"—not right now," she interrupted me. "Not today. But you *are* going. You have to."

"You said that was part of the attraction."

"And it was. Is. You fall for a sailor, you can't be mad when he goes back to sea."

"Am I a sailor or the Scarecrow? We're mixing our myths."

She laughed, and she was so absolutely stunning I said a thing I hadn't expected to say. "It's a big car, Dawn. Seats two, with plenty of space left over. You could take the golden road, too. Take it all the way to the sea. With me."

"Oh, baby boy, you don't mean that. It's sweet, but don't con-fuse a girl."

I took a deep breath and looked out at her golden road. *Did* I mean it?

"Before yesterday," I said, "I had a clear path ahead. Another paycheck or two, and then westward I'd go. Things are less clear today. The boy is as confused as the girl."

We both looked back at the brightening desert plain, and I decided to change the subject. I looked at my watch. "The Red Fox is open. Nothing confusing about coffee and flapjacks."

So we ate breakfast and drank coffee and stared at each other with that comfort and bliss and affection completely unique to a "morning after" with no regrets. We spent the rest of the day in my furnished dump and continued to make up for lost time. We didn't talk about the future, or any yellow-brick or golden roads, or Odysseus and Calypso...

On Monday and Tuesday and Wednesday, she spent the night with me, then slipped out while it was still dark to shower and dress for work at her own home. We kept it cool at the factory, but the boys on the floor knew. They teased me about it, but it wasn't mean. They were envious, sure, but they were also impressed. And they started asking me when I was planning to leave town, which was as charming as it was unsubtle.

Dawn and I made plans to go back to Jerome's on Saturday night.

"Farewell party?" she said, with a sad little smile.

"One-week anniversary," I said, and she laughed and beamed.

Thursday night, she didn't come over. I called her place, and she didn't pick up. I tried not to let my jealous, insecure twenty-two-year-old heart fry my brain. But I also didn't get any sleep.

Friday morning, she wasn't at work. Me and the boys got to it, assembling cubicle walls, but my heart was in my throat. Another cliché, but how else do you say it? My head was pounding. If you can't remember that kind of physical pain, then you don't remember your own fragile young self.

On my first break, I was picking up a payphone to try her at home when the cops walked in.

I hung up without dialing and watched them talk to the receptionist. Saw her point at me. My mind went to the worst thing, but I didn't guess right. There were other bad things it could have been, including at least one that never would have occurred to me.

They held up a picture of a woman with straight dark hair and sad eyes. Black and white, so you couldn't see the blue. But you could see the kindness. They asked the obvious question.

"Of course. That's Dawn, my supervisor. Did something happen to her?"

I got that smug-cop smirk. The "I know something you don't know" smirk. I kept my face blank and impassive.

"She didn't show up to work today. You know anything about that?"

"Nope. She seemed fine yesterday."

"What about last night?" His self-satisfaction was at its peak, but I didn't bite.

"In general, *yesterday* includes a full twenty-four hours. But I didn't see her after work, if that's what you're being cute about."

He didn't like that. He wanted a confession I'd been sleeping with her. "And the night before?"

"The night before, she was her usual happy self. What happened?"

"You her boyfriend?"

"You her mother?" I don't usually mouth off to cops. They have guns and limitless sadism and immunity from any consequences. But a bunch of folks from the floor had stopped work and were watching from a safe distance. I felt like my odds of getting beaten up or killed were slim.

"Listen, asshole. We know you've been sleeping with her. Did she ever tell you her real name's Alice Yvonne Bennett? And she's a fugitive?"

"The one-armed man did it," I said. I couldn't help myself. This was a few years before the big movie, so the cop just got confused and angrier.

"The one-armed—what the fuck are you talking about?"

"Look," I said, taking a deep breath. "I'm sorry. It was a joke. I'm worried about her, and you two aren't making me less worried. What's she wanted for?"

The cops looked at each other. The silent one finally spoke. "Murder. Your girlfriend Dawn, who's really Alice? Well, thing is, she murdered a man and ran away. Still worried about her?"

I played the part of shocked clown for a bit, and they calmed down. It wasn't entirely an act. I could think of reasons why a perfectly good person might run from a murder charge, but did I really want to make excuses without hearing the story from her? Murder was hard to square with the woman I knew—but how well did I really know her? How well does anyone know anyone? Maybe for Dawn-who-was-Alice, the appeal of the golden road was just the appeal of escape.

I finished my day. I gave the front office the address of my old college buddy Bill in Los Angeles to send my last check to. With any luck, I could be on Bill's doorstep before the check hit his mailbox. I knew quitting now would look suspicious, and leaving town only more so. Maybe those two cops and their buddies would chase me to the state line. Maybe they'd check to see if she was in my trunk.

Maybe it would take a little pressure off her if they wasted their time following me.

I didn't care. I hadn't killed anyone, and without Dawn, I was done with this nowhere desert town.

I went back to my furnished dump and packed what little I had. I looked out the window and, sure enough, Tweedledum and Tweedledee had parked their cruiser across the street. Real subtle. Sterling police work.

I thought I was ready to roar off into the desert and leave Dawn behind me. In 1987, there were no cell phones and no internet. If I hit the road, the golden road, that would be it. I would never see her again, never know her story.

That didn't feel right, and I had a hard time accepting it.

Around dusk, I realized where she might be, if she wanted to see me one last time. If she wasn't already halfway to Mexico. First I had to lose the cops. I had an idea about that, too.

They watched me lug my duffel bag out to my car. They watched me leave the key to my dump in the mailbox. I'm sure they were excited. I got in the Impala and took a little tour of the nowhere town. They probably thought I was trying to lose them, but mostly I was trying to bore them.

After about a half hour of meandering, I drove into Reid's junkyard. The cops parked outside the entrance and waited.

Reid was surprised to see me. We didn't like each other. I was playing a hunch, though. His whole operation was shady, and there was no way in the world he liked cops. I told him these two were hassling me. I told him I'd noticed he had a back gate that led to a desert road. He stared at me in silence until I gave him a fifty. He took in the grim visage of President Grant and said, "I'll open the gate. Let me pull my tow truck across the entrance, so they can't see you or follow you through the yard."

I spotted something helpful in his office and bought it for another twenty. Reid was having a big day.

He unlatched the back gate, then went around to fire up his truck. The sun had set. My lights were off. If I could keep off the brakes, they wouldn't see me driving into the desert. If I fought the impulse to speed, they wouldn't see a dust cloud. Reid rolled his tow truck to the front gate, and I pulled slowly out onto the dirt road. I took the time to get out and close the gate behind me, just in case.

The road was ruler-straight for miles. I didn't know how long it would take Tweedledee and Tweedledum to figure out what had happened, but I planned to be invisible long before they did.

A few miles down the road, I looked in the rearview and saw no signs of pursuit. Bless you, Reid. You overcharged for the engine block, but you came through in the end. I'd gambled on him loving a scam, any scam at all, more than he disliked me, and I'd been right.

With the help of a tattered map I'd picked up when I first hit town, I found the Fair Grounds. They were empty, of course. But I parked in roughly the spot I had a week ago, before the stargazing, and sat on the hood of my Impala. And waited.

The Milky Way wheeled slowly overhead. I tried to remember if I'd seen it before, but mostly I thought about the supernova whose name was Dawn or Alice. Dawn the explosion of life and joy, Alice the sad-eyed murderess.

I figured I'd give her until an hour or two after daybreak, then find my way to the closest thick horizontal line on the map and turn west.

It was still full dark when I saw headlights, small and close together. Not a cruiser. More like a VW Bug.

I got off the hood and watched her approach.

Despite everything, her smile was still breathtaking, a supernova by starlight. We didn't embrace. She knew there had to be some talk first.

"I don't know if I'm surprised or not surprised," she said. "I wanted you to be here."

"I wasn't sure you'd want to see me again. But if you did…"

She let it hang there, looked at her feet. "What did they tell you?"

"They told me you killed a man."

She looked up at me. "I did, David. I did that. I won't lie to you."

"There's a lot of reasons a woman kills a man. Which one was it?"

17

"Maybe not the first one that comes to mind."

I mulled that for a minute, then took a stab at it. "So it *wasn't* you? Then who was it? Mother, sister, niece…?"

She looked at the horizon. The light had started to creep over. "You're smart," she said. "I always liked that about you."

"Go on."

She made eye contact again. "I have a sister. She had a husband. She showed up at my house one night, and her face…well, I barely recognized her past the bruises and the blood. I was washing out her wounds when he came pounding on the door and yelling for her." There was a pause. She bit her lip. "I kept a baseball bat by my bed. I went and got it."

"Did he threaten you?"

"He never got a chance to. Swinging the bat at his head was…it wasn't a hard decision. It was no decision at all. It felt good. Overdue. Even when I saw the blood, I didn't stop. I didn't want to stop."

She wasn't emotional about it. I wondered how long ago it had been. The girl in the photo with the dark straight hair looked maybe five years younger. But that didn't matter.

"Was there a trial? Or did you not stick around?"

"I didn't stick around. Her husband was a cop, David. I beat a *cop* to death. So it was another easy decision. I called an ambulance for my sister, kissed her on the forehead, and then—"

"—and then the golden road."

"Something like that," she said. We both looked over at the sunrise. Alice, not Dawn, but also Dawn. She gave a small laugh. "You kill anybody back in Jersey, David?"

"No. I'm one of those idiots who's running away from a perfectly fine life. There might have been an unpaid parking ticket or two." I took a breath. "You could leave the Bug here and get in the Impala."

She smiled again. "I couldn't. You're the sweetest boy, and your future is bright. I'd bring you down, and those dreams of yours…they wouldn't come true. They'd never have a chance."

"I'm tougher than I look. And smart, like you said."

"All that is true. But you didn't sign up for this. I know how you feel right now, but...we just met. Really. You don't owe me the things my troubles would take from you. You owe yourself a new life, like I did when I ran. Chase it. Give it your unlimited devotion and be happy. I'll be okay. I promise."

"Dawn," I started, but it was all I said.

"David." That was all *she* said. But it said everything.

I got my dusty Mets cap from my trunk and handed it to her. "Stuff your hair under that until you have time for a new dye job."

"Yes, sir," she said.

Then I went back into the trunk for the set of license plates I'd bought from Reid and a flathead screwdriver. I replaced the plates on the Bug, while she stared off at the golden road, stretching out to her next new life.

Last kisses are a lot like first kisses.

Anthem of the Sun
Released July 1968

"That's It for the Other One" ("Cryptical Envelopment,"
"Quadlibet for Tenderfeet,"
"The Faster We Go, the Rounder We Get," "We Leave the Castle")
"New Potato Caboose"
"Born Cross-Eyed"
"Alligator"
"Caution (Do Not Stop on Tracks)"

"Cryptical Envelopment" is by Jerry Garcia.
"Quadlibet for Tenderfeet" and
"Caution (Do Not Stop on Tracks)" are by
Garcia, Bill Kreutzmann, Phil Lesh,
Ron "Pigpen" McKernan, and Bob Weir.
"The Faster We Go, the Rounder We Get" is by
Kreutzmann and Weir.
"We Leave the Castle" is by Tom Constanten.
"New Potato Caboose" is by Lesh and Eric Petersen.
"Born Cross-Eyed" is by Weir.
"Alligator" is by Lesh, McKernan, and Robert Hunter.

BORN CROSS-EYED
Linda Landrigan

She wasn't *really* worried about Miss Crowley, Beryl told herself, as she took the exit from the highway for Granville. But she was.

For years, a highlight of her visits home had been a stop on the way out of town to chat with her old fifth-grade teacher at a coffee shop. But on Beryl's last trip to see her parents, the timing hadn't been right to meet. Then she didn't get a birthday card— and Miss Crowley had never missed her birthday in the fifteen or so years since Beryl had been her student. Friends would send her texts and her folks would call, but Miss Crowley always sent an old-fashioned card with a lovely, affirming message that cheered her up.

She'd tried calling from time to time, leaving messages at first, but then she started getting a busy signal. She was a little surprised to realize that she didn't have an email address for the older woman, but then Miss Crowley had never been that forthcoming about herself. Beryl had never even been to her house. Still, she hadn't had such trouble getting in contact before, and now it had been months. So she decided to drop in and check on her old teacher. For an excuse, she brought along some books on art therapy that she thought Miss Crowley would like.

All through elementary school, the other kids had called Beryl "Gladly" because of her one crossed eye. She had been a bit of an outcast, shy and awkward. Then, in fifth grade, she had found a friend in Miss Crowley, who would sit with her on a bench at recess and listen to her recite her fears and concerns, never belittling them as other adults would. It was Miss Crowley who had inspired Beryl to go into social work and to focus on kids who had some disfiguring disability.

After college, she started meeting up occasionally with her old teacher over coffee, sharing light gossip and reminiscences over lattes and bagels. Miss Crowley gave Beryl the advice that helped her land her first job and the wisdom that helped her navigate life as a new adult. "Don't pick at your scabs," was one tidbit she'd needed to hear when she was still visited by memories of old taunts and hurts.

It turned out Miss Crowley lived in a neighborhood Beryl didn't know very well. The streets ran like squiggles, and after driving around and not finding the right one, she wondered if the very private Miss Crowley had even put the correct address on the envelopes in which her birthday cards had arrived. She pulled over and dug her phone out of her backpack to look it up on the maps app—but she'd forgotten to charge the thing before leaving her parents' house. She would just have to pull into a stranger's driveway and ask someone...except the houses had their blinds closed, their driveways empty. Everyone seemed to be at work.

Beryl sighed. Probably Miss Crowley was out as well. If she managed to find the house, she would leave the books at the door with a "Sorry to miss you" note. Just as she was about to turn around, she saw the sign for Morning Lane.

Miss Crowley's house sat up a bit, obscured by unpruned hedges, and looked as asleep as all the others. Beryl found a safe place to pull over and had an odd sense of déjà vu. Once she'd been in the car with her father, driving along a winding, deserted street like this one. Coming to a sudden stop, he had banged his fists on the steering wheel and started to cry. It must have been about the time she was starting middle school. Beryl had been frightened by her father's outburst, and—she was ashamed to admit to herself now—a bit disgusted. But his fit was brief, and then he drove on home.

Beryl shoved the memory to the back of her mind as she peeled herself out of the car and grabbed her backpack. She was met on the porch by a dirty, skinny black-and-white cat that rubbed against her legs as she waited for Miss Crowley to answer the door.

"You're a friendly guy. Are you a stray?" she said, squatting down to pet the cat, who purred as if Beryl had something to feed him. Her hands came away greasy and smelly. Something twitched inside her then—her social-worker sense that something was off. Stepping down from the porch, she saw the cat trot around the corner of the house and followed him to the back door, where he slipped through a ragged slit in the screen.

Approaching it, the first thing Beryl noticed was that, despite the chill in the air, the inside door was open to the kitchen, and the screen door was the only barrier to the house.

"Hello? Miss Crowley? I'm looking for Lois Crowley!" she shouted. She tried the door, but it was latched. After calling out once more, she worked her fingers through a tear in the upper part of the screen and unlatched the door.

She sensed no movement in the house, only the cat sitting on the counter, looking at her quizzically. She called out again, this time adding, "Wellness check! Hello?"

The kitchen smelled musty. Dirty dishes sat by the sink. The faucet had a slow drip. A large bag of cat food sat on a case of sodas. It appeared to have been clawed open; bits of kibble spilled out and were strewn around the floor. Beryl noticed another bag lying empty in a corner, and on one of the chairs still another, this one unopened. She flicked the light switch, but nothing happened. She checked the wall phone. The line was dead.

In the dining room, the musty smell was worse. The table was strewn with newspaper clippings, some with names highlighted in yellow, and on one corner sat a stack of library books. Beryl checked their due dates: all May. They were months overdue.

To the right was an office with a desk under the window; on it were more clippings held down with a snow globe and an old-fashioned Selectric typewriter. Beside that were three neatly stacked reams of paper. Miss Crowley apparently liked to buy in bulk.

At the far end of the dining room, a hallway led to the front door and stairs. The cat ran down the hall and scurried up the stairs, apparently familiar with the house. Beryl knocked on a closed door at the end of the hall and called out before pushing it open.

Immediately, the smell became something much worse. She stepped in, her eyes sweeping the floor, expecting to find a dead dog, but what she saw sent her running to the kitchen to heave over the sink. Sitting in a chair facing the door were the desiccated remains of her friend and mentor, Lois Crowley.

After a few minutes, Beryl came back to her senses. She reached for her phone but remembered she'd let the battery run down. She looked out the window at the sleeping house next door, then twisted her head to glance up the empty street.

After a few more deep breaths, she decided to brave another look at the body. She reached into her backpack for a face mask she'd tucked in there.

Approaching cautiously, she stood at the door to take stock of what she was seeing. Miss Crowley was wearing a tweed skirt, cream-colored blouse, and light blue cardigan. Her feet were planted in pink bunny slippers, a fashion choice Beryl would never have guessed. Her hands rested on a magazine on her lap; it appeared to be a *New Yorker*.

Beryl looked at the sweater, which didn't seem to have been punctured by anything like a knife or bullet. Nor was there any stain on the wall behind the chair to indicate blood splatter. Wiry brown hair was falling off the skull, but from where she stood

Beryl could see no indication that someone might have knocked the woman over the head. It appeared that Miss Crowley had simply died while reading her magazine.

Horrified yet unable to take her eyes off the corpse, she backed out of the living room and considered what to do. She would have to call the police, of course. And do something about the cat. It must have been Miss Crowley's, able to survive only because the teacher happened to have a leaky sink and had bought cat food in bulk. Perhaps she'd better sort the cat first, in case the police objected to her taking it. Poor Miss Crowley wasn't going anywhere. Wondering if there were any other pets in the house, Beryl followed the cat upstairs.

On the upper landing, she cracked open a window and inhaled fresh, cool air before exploring the bedrooms. She opened a linen closet, and bundles of toilet paper rained down, revealing bottles of hand lotion, multiple boxes of toothpaste, and, behind two bags of kitty litter, a cat carrier. Beryl pulled it out; it had *Tommy* written on top in magic marker.

Beyond the bathroom was a bedroom, apparently a spare being used for storage. It was stuffed with boxes and bags of things bought in bulk: paper towels, toilet paper, garbage bags. Plastic bins held pocketbooks and clothes—some with their price tags still attached. On a side table was a sewing machine and a stack of old pattern catalogues, probably picked up in a used bookstore. There was a box of canning jars and lids, a set of sheets still in their plastic packaging, cardboard boxes stacked upon each other and nearly tumbling over.

Beryl pondered how much she didn't know about the woman downstairs, her friend. Miss Crowley had been a hoarder, too embarrassed perhaps by the state of her house to have anyone come over. That's why she'd always suggested meeting Beryl at a coffee shop, always someplace close to the interstate so Beryl wouldn't have to drive through town. As far as Beryl knew, she had no immediate family, so who was going to go through all this stuff?

***

Continuing to poke around, Beryl ended up in the master bedroom. The bed was made but muddled with cat hair, in the middle of which Tommy had settled, as if waiting for Beryl to come and comfort him.

"You're a resourceful fella, Tommy, to survive here," she said, and he heaved himself up and rubbed against her, leaving a swath of fur. "Did Miss Crowley retire? Didn't *anyone* notice she'd quit showing up in town? Oh, Tommy, I had no idea."

She walked to the dresser: chunky costume jewelry piled onto a necklace tree, a plain Timex watch, more hand lotion. Tucked into the mirror frame were a couple of faded baseball cards. But, Beryl noted, no family pictures.

She timidly pulled open the top drawer and found a tangle of more costume jewelry. A box of lace-edged handkerchiefs, unopened. A pixie case of glittery eyeshadow, of a type Miss Crowley never wore.

The teacher had always been particularly kind to Beryl. When the other kids were making fun of her at recess, Miss Crowley would pull her aside and sit with her and let her talk about the things that made her sad—the other kids taunting her about her eye, her parents fighting over her dad's drinking, their old car that kept breaking down, not being able to go to summer camp like her classmates...

Miss Crowley was kind and sympathetic and lovely, with auburn hair that she kept in a loose bun at the back of her neck. She would brush Beryl's hair out of her eyes and tell her she was special and had an artist's eye.

She taught Beryl to draw, so she could park herself in a corner during recess and have something to do instead of fretting that she was left out of the other kids' games. She was the reason Beryl had studied art in college, the reason she'd become a social worker.

"Oh, Miss Crowley," Beryl sighed. "I'm so sorry. I'll try to make amends. I'll take care of Tommy and let the police know, so you can have a decent burial and all."

Beryl knew she had to get out of there, yet she was reluctant to say goodbye. She wrestled Tommy into his carrier and carted him downstairs. She set him by the back door and made one more pass through the house.

She was getting used to the smell now and found she could just tolerate sitting across the room from Miss Crowley.

"I'm sorry I never asked about *you*," she said. "I always did all the talking—like now, I suppose. And I will let people know. I'll call the superintendent's office." Perched on the edge of a chair, Beryl felt like an awkward schoolgirl all over again. Tommy howled.

"Well, I'd best be going." Beryl slapped her thighs, stood up, and stepped out of the room, taking a shallow breath.

Passing by the office, she decided to take a closer look. There was the table and typewriter. And opposite that, a bookshelf of children's and young-adult books. Beryl ran her hands over the spines and noted a few of her own favorites, ones Miss Crowley had loaned her and never minded whether they came back or not. She always seemed to have just the right book for the moment, Beryl remembered.

With all the books and paper, the room felt more like a library, and it did seem to invite one to explore. Beryl was struck just then by the presence of the typewriter. Was Miss Crowley writing something? Her own YA book, perhaps? Was that why she was saving all the newspaper clippings, as research for her fictional world? To the side of the desk was a file cabinet, its top drawer ajar. Thinking she could save whatever it was Miss Crowley was working on, Beryl pulled open the drawer.

It was stuffed with files, alphabetized by last names. Her first thought was that Miss Crowley had kept files on her students, and she started to close the drawer. But then a name jumped out at her. Dabowski. There had been a family down her street with that name; they were friends with her parents and came over often. Beryl remembered now: they had a sweet little boy about five who had an imaginary pony he said followed him everywhere. But they'd moved away, and at some point her parents had lost contact with them.

Beryl pulled out the file. Inside was a smudged carbon copy of a letter: "Dear Mrs. Dabowski, You are too old to be dressing like a teenager. People around here are talking about your short skirts and skimpy tops that leave little to the imagination. Just think what a negative impact this will have on little Joel's psychological development." It was signed, "Someone Who Has Studied Child Psychology."

Beryl chuckled ruefully. Apparently, Miss Crowley could be something of a busybody. She looked at the date of the letter. Little Joel would have been about seven or eight. She didn't imagine Caroline Dabowski taking such a letter to heart, nor did she remember the woman dressing particularly inappropriately. Well, Miss Crowley was from a different generation.

She reached for another file. "Dear Mr. Weisman," began a letter addressed to the president of the Crown Savings and Loan. "Your loan officer, Miles Gardner, has a dangerous gambling problem. He has emptied his savings and blown through his wife's inheritance. He's desperate, and he'll start robbing the till at the bank soon to feed his addiction. Sincerely, A Concerned Customer."

She flipped through the files and drew another from the middle of the drawer. "Dear Mr. Picard, It has come to my attention that our city comptroller, Harold Grahame, has been dipping his fingers into the pot and spending our money on his mistress." This one was signed, "A Concerned Taxpayer Who Happens to Know." Stapled to the letter were a series of ten-year-old newspaper articles about the corrupt comptroller. Beryl remembered the scandal, remembered her grandparents' outrage at the lack of oversight when the news broke that he'd been arrested.

Beryl pulled out another file and fanned through the letters it held. The top one was addressed to a Mrs. Liu. It said, "I feel you should know that your daughter-in-law is having an affair with a younger man who works with her at the gallery." It was signed "A Friend Who Cares."

She recalled the minister of their church, who'd had a messy divorce. His daughter was one of the kids who'd teased Beryl the most at school. Thomas? Thompson? Tamsin! She reached for the Ts and pulled out a file; once again she found a stack of yellowed newspaper clippings, the last of which was a notice of his death by suicide.

Beryl pulled out the bottom drawer and looked for her own name, and there it was: Wiest.

Her hands shook as she held a faded piece of paper dated some fifteen years ago, when she had still been Miss Crowley's student.

"To Whom It May Concern: I have it on good authority that the lead technical researcher in your bioinformatics division, Bernard Wiest, plagiarized his last published article, of which I've attached a copy. Moreover, his drinking off the job is affecting his judgment. He should not drink and drive!"

Beryl thought back to those last days. Her father *had* been drinking a lot, and he *had* lost his job, had been devastated by the loss of his source of income. They'd sold the house and moved in with Beryl's grandparents. Her father quit drinking and got another job, but he was never quite the same. Still, she was certain he would never have plagiarized another's work. Clipped to the letter was a photocopy of the contents page of a scientific journal, but there was no other evidence in the file.

Beryl had confided in Miss Crowley about her parents' problems, as she as an eleven-year-old kid had understood them—but, really, would Miss Crowley have written that letter? She didn't want to believe it.

She flung the file to the floor and snatched others at random. There were hundreds of poison-pen letters, dating back years.

They targeted prominent people and ordinary folks alike. Like Professor Sheila Listen—Beryl's heart sank when she found that file. It was she who'd told Miss Crowley about taking a walk on the beach at night and seeing her French professor with one of her classmates. At the time, Beryl had merely thought it was funny. But Miss Crowley's letter to the dean of the arts and sciences division of her college called the act "predatory and inappropriate."

She looked at the piles of paper now scattered about. All these people's lives upended, and why? And what if anything should—*could*—she do about it now? When she'd faced a dilemma in the past, Beryl had always brought it to Miss Crowley, but now?...

She stood up and walked back to the living room. "Why, Miss C?" she said aloud to the empty room. "Is this how you filled your lonely hours? Did it give you a sense of power? Did you think you were changing the course of history in some small way? Oh, never mind. You don't have to tell me why."

Tommy took up howling again, and Beryl realized what she had to do. She went to the kitchen and located some matches in a drawer. Then she returned to the office and pulled the rest of the files from the cabinet. She piled Miss Crowley's life's work together on the floor and set the papers on fire.

She picked up Tommy's carrier on her way out of the house.

The neighborhood was still deserted as she drove away, and only when she stopped to fill her gas tank at the edge of town did she see traffic reviving. The sound of sirens filled the air, and she looked in the direction of Miss Crowley's house.

A tendril of black smoke was reaching for the clouds.

"Goodbye, Miss C," she whispered. "Goodbye, goodbye, good-bye."

Aoxomoxoa
Released June 1969

"St. Stephen"
"Dupree's Diamond Blues"
"Rosemary"
"Doin' That Rag"
"Mountains of the Moon"
"China Cat Sunflower"
"What's Become of the Baby"
"Cosmic Charlie"

"St. Stephen" was written by
Jerry Garcia, Phil Lesh, and Robert Hunter.
All other songs are by Garcia and Hunter.

WHAT'S BECOME OF THE BABY
Dominique Biebau
translated from the Flemish by Josh Pachter

In every river, there are beings that envy our ability to breathe. Some people claim that the Molenvliet—the river that cuts through the middle of our village—provides a home to creatures that only emerge at night. Their voices drive travelers mad and attempt to seduce them beneath the surface of the water.

Pieter always laughed when he heard these old wives' tales. That was my brother for you: there was only room in his head for facts and figures. Credits, debits, and—perhaps most important—the difference between them, which was what kept increasing his wealth.

The river was his most important employee. Its current turned the mill's waterwheel, and that's where his money came from, all summer long. The farmers brought their grain from kilometers away, and grinding it into flour turned Pieter's jet-black hair gray and spread a downy white blanket across the interior of the mill. During the warm summer months, the mill was a lively place, with the rasping of the wheel and the voices of our customers, their throats and wallets loosened by smooth Dutch gin.

In the summer, when the fields grew fat in the rhythm of the sun, you might think of the river as a friend, a troubadour whose gentle song accompanied the life of the village. Only in the autumn, when thunderstorms caused the water to spill over the river's banks and relentlessly pounded the wheel in violet waves, did the Molenvliet reveal its true colors. It shrugged off its chains and bucked like an angry bull against the banks that held it captive. At night, my fellow villagers lit candles at the feet of the statue of St. Stephen, the patron saint of bricklayers and stonemasons, praying for the storms to abate and the water to return to its usual calm. Little did they know...

For me, the true horror began in the winter, when panes of crystal ice hid the Molenvliet beneath their sparkling surface. That's when I heard the voices.

I always used to wear white dresses, and my laughter was loud and frequent. Dressed in white and laughing, I strolled our village streets. I sang, too: old songs no one had taught me. And I told stories the villagers had long since forgotten. Of course there were eyes that watched me pass, most of them misty with emotion, because they saw in me—just for a moment—another, more beautiful world.

Other eyes were less kind. There are always some people who see beauty and think only of possessing it, see flowers and think only of plucking them.

And one day I, too, was plucked.

Some people say that ice has no smell, but they're mistaken. It smells of fear and grief—and blood.

I no longer wore white dresses. And that's not the only thing I stopped doing. I no longer sang. I sat in my room and listened to my brother and Ellen, his bride, fight—mostly about me. I sat on my bed and stared straight before me, my eyes narrowed, as if focused on something that wasn't even there. If I looked closely enough, though, perhaps I would finally be able to see the past.

But my efforts produced no results. A stubborn quilt with the weight of a thousand tears covered my memories, the elusive remnants of forgotten dreams.

Ellen was always kind to me. Sometimes she brought me a little something extra to nibble on—a piece of sugarloaf, a slice of cake. In exchange for her kindness, I would tell her one of my stories, one of the ones I still remembered. She liked ghost stories best, full of blood and looming creatures. Sometimes I looked anxiously at the baby sleeping peacefully in his crib. When Ellen noticed, she smiled. "Are you afraid your stories will harm my baby?" she asked.

I nodded.

"But everything's fine so far," she said. "Isn't it?"

So far. She attached those two words to all the shadows in the room. I thought back to when we were both pregnant, both filled with hope for the future.

I thought of Lukas.

They found me late one night a kilometer outside the village, lying on the ice, in a spot where the Molenvliet had risen several meters above its banks, like a clenched fist. No one could say how long I'd been there or how I'd come to be there. It was a miracle I hadn't fallen through the ice and drowned.

It was Pieter who found me. His warm hands lifted me to my feet. "What happened, sister?" he whispered in my ear. "In the name of God, what happened?"

I felt frozen, as if an icicle had grown within me.

"The baby," I said. "What's become of the baby?" I rested my palms on my belly and felt nothing.

Only then did I see the red stains on the ice. Pieter put his

37

hands over my eyes.

"What happened?" he repeated, more emphatically this time.

I shook my head. "I don't know," I stammered.

Pieter's strong arms—miller's arms—carried me back to the village. All the way, I fixed my gaze behind us. A chorus of dead souls droned from beneath the ice, a skein of voices that included that of my stillborn child.

I'd known Lukas since we were children. His mother never breastfed him, so he was always a sickly boy, fragile, pale as milky glass. But his mind sparkled like water in the sun. Because his hands were too delicate for a farmer's life, his father apprenticed him to a weaver, so he would learn a trade. When his apprenticeship ended, we married.

There are two types of people: those who look into the water, and like Narcissus, see only a reflection of themselves, and those who, in its depths, discover new realities.

Lukas lived with his eyes wide open. He belonged to the kingdom of ghosts and mythical creatures, the land where writers and poets abide. He told me wonderful stories, and I gave him my music and my body. We were happy, an emotion that only grew stronger when we learned I was pregnant.

Not long after that, it turned out that Ellen was also with child. Everything was perfect for all of us.

Until that one bloody night.

The gentleness that had attracted me to Lukas turned out to be his downfall. What happened to me that night drove him mad, and two days after I lost my baby, a new singer joined the underwater choir.

Ever since the birth of his son, Pieter wanted me gone. "She's been touched by Death," I once overheard him say to Ellen. "That can't be good for our boy."

38

I was standing at the head of the stairs, about to come down, but when I heard those words, I froze. I wasn't ready to leave the Molenvliet behind.

Ellen's voice, clear but faint, drifted up from below. "Leave her be, Pieter. She helps keep me from being bored. She tells lovely stories. Please, Pieter...for a while longer."

I could imagine the way she looked, a fragile statue of resistance.

"But we could turn her room into a nursery. And she can go to the Magdalene sisters. They accept fallen women."

Ellen's resolve remained firm. "She's not a fallen woman. She was married, and her husband and baby died. Perhaps when our son is a little older. Right now, her grief is much too fresh."

I coughed, so they would know I could hear them. Pieter had the decency to close his eyes and change the subject.

Later, I heard him throw a tantrum in the mill room. He slammed doors and flung sacks of flour against the wall. I wasn't the only dangerous occupant of that house.

When Lukas died, I stopped singing. I tried once, but my voice was so scratchy I wept in frustration. I traded my white dresses for black ones. "The Crow," the villagers began to call me. "The Mill Crow."

It didn't bother me.

A few days after my miscarriage, Ellen gave birth to her little boy. It went as such things always go in Molenvliet: quickly and without much of a fuss.

Pieter later told anyone who would listen how he'd heard a sudden scream from the stables and ran cursing, his hands dusted with flour, to find Ellen lying in a pool of blood with a squalling infant in her arms. The new mother had cut the umbilical cord herself. He always ended the story the same way:

"Our Molenvliet women are as hard as ice."

I missed out on the birth. I was a ghost, locked in my room, swaying between life and death.

Pieter called his son Gideon, a Leysen family name that went back several generations. He invited all the region's farmers to toast the child's health. Even I was handed a glass of table beer. I was an island of silence amongst the exuberant company.

In the middle of the crowd sat the new mother, a pale Madonna, her baby boy on her lap. She looked exhausted, with black circles under her eyes. Pieter stood beside her, strong and healthy as ever, a proud papa—yet clearly aware of the potential financial benefit of the occasion.

What wouldn't I have given to see Lukas there in Pieter's place? That thought filled me with horror. How could I be so inconsiderate of my own brother, the man who had rescued me from an icy death?

Suddenly there was a commotion. Ellen had taken ill. Two of the farmers' wives supported her on either side and led her to her bedroom. I took charge of Gideon. The baby purred with pleasure, but Pieter saw us and pulled the lad away from me.

"Don't you *touch* my son," he snarled.

He glared at me, his eyes aflame. I didn't understand his anger, but from that day forward, I was never permitted to come anywhere near little Gideon.

Gideon was a sickly child. Ellen wasn't producing milk, and she tried to feed the boy cow's milk, but that didn't satisfy him. He cried a lot. Once I suggested that I could nurse him: my own breasts still strained with milk. But Ellen refused with a stubbornness I wasn't accustomed to seeing in her. "My child," she insisted. "My milk."

Ever since she became a mother, the distance between us had widened.

At least I still had my stories. Like a clever Scheherazade, I tempted her with tales I always broke off before the end. In this way, I bound our lives together with words. But I had no illusions. My skill as a storyteller was the only thing that kept me out of the convent.

Life went on. Despite the traumatic events, I seemed to achieve a sort of balance.

But when Gideon turned two, something unanticipated happened. Ellen proposed that we go for a walk. "Some fresh air will do us both good," she said.

We left Gideon in the care of a neighbor and strolled beside the Molenvliet. It was November, and in some places the river had already overflowed its banks. We carefully navigated around the occasional pools of stagnant water. And eventually we came to the place where I had been found unconscious on the ice. I wanted to move on as quickly as possible, but Ellen held me back.

"What do you remember about that night?" she asked. We stood in the shadow of a willow whose branches brushed the ground. Ellen's pale face shone like a death mask in the darkness that surrounded us. I didn't know how to answer her question.

And then she grabbed my wrists with surprising strength. "What—do—you—remember?" she repeated, emphasizing each word.

"Nothing," I gasped. "Absolutely nothing. I fell, and then—I woke up on the ice. Pieter found me. Please let me go."

My response seemed to calm Ellen. Her expression softened. "I'm sorry," she said, and I believed she meant it. "This place—there's blood here. Terrible things happened here. Let's go home."

On the way, I told her the story of Medea, a mother who murdered her own children rather than allow her ex-husband to raise them.

"What a horrible woman!" She shivered, but her eyes glistened with excitement.

**

That night, I lay with my ear to the floor of my room and listened to the voices that drifted up from below—not so different in tone from the voices in the water.

"She has to go," hissed Pieter, and this time there was no answering protest.

I pressed the side of my head harder against the floorboards.

"I'm going to Vereeckens tomorrow to fetch pork lard to grease the millstones," I heard my brother say. "That takes me right past the convent. Mother Superior still owes me some money. With a little luck, I'll convince her to take Lore in."

The convent. The thought of it stabbed into me like needles. The Magdalene sisters were known for their rough treatment of their sinful "guests." Long days slaving in the laundry. Both physical and mental abuse. And I would be leaving forever the place where I once was happy, the place where I heard the echoing voices of those I had lost. It would be the death of me.

I awoke very early. It had snowed during the night, and the Molenvliet lurked beneath a coat of frozen armor. It was still cold. I went outside and hid in the stable, waiting for Pieter to come and saddle his horse. I prepared myself to deliver a plea that would melt the polished ice caverns of my brother's heart.

When I stepped out of the shadows, he clutched a hand to his heart. "Lore," he said. "You startled me." He looked as if he'd seen a ghost.

"Don't do it," I whispered.

He didn't take my meaning at first, but then his expression hardened. He turned his back on me and hoisted his saddle.

"Don't send me away, brother!" That last word made him hesitate for a moment, but then he led his horse outside. I followed him and laid a hand on his shoulder. He wrenched away, and I lost my balance and tumbled headlong into the snow.

Dazed, I felt him lift me from the ground—just as he'd done that fatal night on the river—and carry me to my room. He laid me on my bed and closed the door behind him when he left. The sound of a key turning in the lock confirmed my suspicions. I was a prisoner.

From my window, I watched Pieter spur his horse and disappear in the direction of the village.

I wept and brushed the snow from my hair. The smell of fresh-fallen snow awakened memories within me. For the first time, the blanket that had long hidden those memories from my sight was ripped aside. I opened the window and listened to the voices arise from the water.

We stroll beside the river, Ellen and me, our bulging bellies hidden beneath loose maternity dresses. We waddle like old ducks through the snow. It's cold, the frozen Molenvliet not yet cracking. The wind takes hold of our skirts and shakes them.

"Pieter is so eager to have a child," Ellen says.

I smile. I know my brother well enough to know that what Ellen says isn't entirely true. Pieter is eager to have a son, *someone he can entrust the mill to when his hair is gray year-round.*

"Would you like to see something?" asks Ellen, and she raises the hem of her dress.

"I don't know if," I begin, but she waves away my objection.

"Look," she says. The word is no longer an invitation but a command. The thick woolen fabric rises past her waist.

A pillow falls to the snow, and I stare a question at her.

"I lost it," she says. "Yesterday. There was blood on my sheets. I burned them. And the rest, I—I threw into the water." She stares at me with huge feverish eyes. "I'm afraid there's something wrong with me, and I can never have children. Pieter will leave me." She gestures shyly at my belly. "Can I have—your baby? You're still young."

Her suggestion is so ridiculous, I have to laugh. Ellen's face changes, and a second Ellen appears, one who's lived in her body for years but I've never before seen. Her pupils contract, and she spits like a lizard. "I need your baby, Lore."

She produces a knife.

I fall from the path onto the ice.

I pulled hopelessly at the door of my room, pounded on the walls, stamped on the floor. Ellen didn't react. And why should she? I leaned out of the window and considered jumping. Then I saw them, two black shadows in a white world. Ellen had taken Gideon outside, far from the racket his real mother was making. They were playing in the snow on the other side of the Molenvliet. Ellen threw snowballs at Gideon, who ran in laughing circles in an attempt to avoid them.

It should have been *me* playing with him.

After an hour, they both collapsed at the foot of a crooked alder and stretched out in the evening sun like lazy cats. The ice on the river cracked. The thaw had begun.

I leaned out my window and sang, and my voice had returned to its former power. Gideon looked up, surprised, but Ellen slept on, a satisfied smile on her face.

This was my chance.

I sang the songs I had never forgotten, songs of longing and loss, of birth and death, of a never-ending always, of the paradise that lay just beyond the next hill. I imagined that the ghosts in the river were listening. Did they brush tears from their eyes? Did they still have hearts?

Gideon stood, transfixed by the strange songs that echoed from the house. With a face as perfect as the dawn, he turned homeward and began his final walk. Every step brought him closer to the river. I sang.

"You delightful child, come with me," I sang. The words were Goethe's, from his ballad *The Erl-King*, but I sang them as if I had written them myself. "I'll play wonderful games with you.

Colorful flowers grow on the shore."

The ice cracked. I jumped. I flew, then fell like a songbird frozen in its flight.

And two new voices joined the river choir.

Workingman's Dead
Released June 1970

"Uncle John's Band"
"High Time"
"Dire Wolf"
"New Speedway Boogie"
"Cumberland Blues"
"Black Peter"
"Easy Wind"
"Casey Jones"

"Cumberland Blues" is by Jerry Garcia,
Phil Lesh, and Robert Hunter.
"Easy Wind" is by Hunter.
All other songs are by Garcia and Hunter.

DIRE WOLF
Vinnie Hansen

When I set out to kill John, I had plenty of reasons. He'd stolen my song, crushed my soul, and was en route to crushing my kid sister Carmelita's, too.

I spun my wheels in doubt, of course. Me, Carrie Cunningham, a demure former music major—I suffered self-doubt in spades. A whole *deck* of spades. After all, if I'd had any confidence, I never would have stuck with John for all those years. And, yes, the prospect of prison was a deterrent.

But after struggling out of the mire of self-doubt, I started planning.

John and I weren't married.

We were in a band together, Dire Wolf. Not the one in New York that's *just* a cover band; the one from the Bay Area that mixes Dead covers with some originals, including our almost famous "Maybe."

The five of us knew each other better than many married couples do. We practiced together, were on the road together, performed together. We shared bad food, inside jokes, and our own language. When John touched his index finger to his forehead, we went to the top of the song. If he spun the finger, we tagged the line.

And like any dysfunctional family of five, we fought.

"I *am* Dire Wolf," John said. We were doing our sound check at a dinky Fresno venue, because that's the kind of gig we got. He tapped the mic, dented from his drops. It shrilled.

"Dire wolves are extinct," I said pointedly.

I hit an A on my keyboard for Michael. His lanky body stooped over a turquoise Stratocaster. Knobby fingers turned a peg.

I pounded the A again. Michael and I both enjoyed the moment, because tuning bugged the shit out of John.

"Babe," John said—it had taken me a ridiculously long time to realize that wasn't a pet name for me but what he called all women—"don't be so literal. 'Dire Wolf' is a Grateful Dead song."

As if I didn't know.

Riley and Fred chortled, because they were both baked. They were also both bald—Riley by choice, Fred by age. Both stood about five-ten and were broad-shouldered, which might have been confusing from the back, except Riley ran toward tight jeans in bright colors and sleeveless shirts that showed off his ripped drummer arms, while Fred, our bassist, dressed as if he were in the actual Grateful Dead.

John's comment prompted Fred to play the four-note lead-in to "Dire Wolf," and Riley joined with drums. Together, they created our band's steady bottom. John picked up his guitar, more a prop than an instrument. He sang with a buttery tenor, a voice that caused women to toss doobies onto the stage—not to this Dead tune about a drunk addressing a phantasmagoric wolf but to *my* song.

"Maybe" was our only original ever to get major airtime. A set closer. A song John had appropriated as his own. Nobody heard "Maybe" and thought of me.

At the front of the stage, John leaned in, eating the mic, his still-fine tush outlined by purple pants.

I blame *that* moment and Robert Hunter's lyrics for planting the idea of murder, of John kissing some undetectable poison off the microphone's grill.

He'd barely finished his second time through the chorus when he stopped cold and said, "Can we get rid of that goddamn ground hum?" He spun toward me, not because he expected me to fix the problem, but because I tickled the ivories in the back, where all the equipment plugged in.

Michael didn't say anything. He never spoke to John if he could help it, since he regarded him as a womanizing pig. Silently, he parked his guitar in its stand, rummaged in a black bag full of cables and cords and splitters, and came up with an adapter. He plugged the amp into it, then plugged the adapter into the outlet.

I'd seen him do this many times before but saw it now with fresh eyes. "Isn't that dangerous?"

Michael gave me a squinty-eyed look. "I do it every single time John gets a bug up his ass about the hum."

"Right." I noodled a progression of arpeggiated chords. *Time to shut up.* I wasn't going to be an idiot like the man who Googled "how to dispose of a hundred-and-twenty-pound body" and then offed his hundred-and-twenty-pound wife.

Fred repeated the pickup, and Riley and John restarted "Dire Wolf."

With a downward stroke of his arm, John cut them off. He whirled toward Michael and me. Snapped his fingers. "You two can start participating any time now."

I ran the backs of my fingernails up the keyboard, offering a loud glissando in retort.

When we finished running through the song, John glanced up to a windowed room in the back. The club's sound engineer gave a thumbs up. "Let's try our softer side," John said, unhooking the mic. We all knew this meant "Maybe."

I played my intro solo. The A-minor riff haunted my bones. It carried memories of the first time, me at the piano and John cross-legged on the floor of my bedroom, an acoustic guitar cradled in his lap. Back then, John nodded his head enthusiastically when I finished. "That's fricking fantastic."

His approval had fluttered through me, better even than our first sex.

"I think we have a hit," he said.

I hadn't minded the "we."

Then.

Now, as the band snuck in and John began to croon, I almost cried. "Maybe" was *my* song. When John first posted it to the streaming services, it had made sense to use his accounts. He was the only person in the band with a significant number of followers.

Who knew then that one of them was an influencer who would fall in love with "Maybe"? The money trickled in at first, so I didn't protest. But then it became a steady flow.

To John.

It wasn't enough to make anyone rich. John still lived in the same almost-nice apartment, but he drove a new Tesla. When I protested, he said, "They're *my* followers, babe."

Our band didn't have the money for a driver or roadie. After two forty-five-minute sets, we loaded the van ourselves, and Michael drove to our crusty Fresno hotel—two adjoining rooms, each with two queen beds. He was a little too old and a lot too drunk for the two-and-a-half-hour truck back to Santa Cruz.

Michael and I—united in our antipathy toward John—shared one room, and Riley and Fred took the other. John hadn't returned with us. He'd "gotten lucky" again.

Which brings me to my other reason for wanting him dead. Bad enough that John had broken my heart—Carmelita's was next. When I'd tried to broach the subject of John's infidelity with my little sister—now John's significant other—Carmelita had said, "I can take care of myself" and hung up on me.

In our hotel room, Michael raised a half-empty bottle of Jack Daniels in one hand, a vial of Ambien in the other. He washed a pill down with a swig of whiskey, winked, and plopped into bed.

Next door, Fred ran through a bass line. My ears perked. I didn't recognize it. *Intriguing. Insistent. Minor key, but melodious.*

When Michael was finally snoring, I pressed my ear to the adjoining door. By then, only cannabis fumes and silence leaked around the edges.

Slipping along the hall, I rode the elevator down to the lobby, where two computers in an alcove made up their "business center." An anonymous place for some research.

Electrocution on stage.

I clicked "Top 5 Most Shocking Deaths—The Show Won't Go On."

In the Seventies, a keyboard player named Aleksander Ilic had started a rock band in Yugoslavia. He called it *San*, which meant "dream." A few years into their success, their lead singer grabbed an ungrounded mic—and bye-bye dream.

In 1972, Stone the Crows' lead guitarist Les Harvey joined the "27 Club" of Janis, Jimi, and other famous musicians who died at that unfortunate age when he grabbed an improperly grounded mic in front of twelve hundred fans in Swansea, Wales.

So it *had* happened.

And it could happen again.

When John invited me into Dire Wolf, I was nineteen. He was twenty-nine. Carmelita was twelve. She adored him. He sang to her, twirled her about my apartment, called her "Man Slayer." When he broke my heart, he broke hers, too. But I remained in the band. Because being in a band was all I'd ever wanted, and this one worked.

Carmelita sprouted into a vibrant, stunning young woman, and John took note. He serenaded her in the front row. With *my* song.

I tried to warn her.

"You had your chance," she said.

True.

"Me and John are not you and John."

True.

"You always treat me like a little sister."

True.

"I'm entitled to my own mistakes."

True.

I backed off, not wanting to cause a rift too deep to cross.

In two months, they were living together. Now, two years later, I'd reached a tipping point. I could forgive John for cheating on me, even for keeping the money earned by my song, but not for cheating on Carmelita.

I stood up from the computer, stretched, and turned into the short hotel hallway to catch the elevator, nearly colliding with John.

"Hey, babe," he said. "Burning the midnight oil?" We entered the elevator. He swayed toward me and caught himself on my shoulder. A miasma of odors wafted from his half-buttoned shirt—sweat, cigarettes, and deceit.

"Writing a song," I said.

He straightened, eyes suddenly alert.

"'Midnight Oil in Fresno,'" I said.

"Funny."

The elevator dinged.

As John fumbled with his key card, I entered my room. Michael was flopped stomach down, sleeping the sleep of those not planning murder. I lifted the keys to the van from his pants pocket and the complimentary make-up-remover pad from the bathroom.

Though we took our instruments into our rooms with us, our less valuable equipment remained in the van. I scooted onto the back bench seat and found the mic's XLR cable. Then I fished around for the little tool kit Michael kept under the seat.

It might sound like I knew what I was doing. Not really.

The internet had informed me that, if an amp is ungrounded—as John's was likely to be whenever, as Michael put it, he got "a bug up his ass about the hum"—it could harbor stray AC voltage. If you were playing guitar, the strings would make you part of the circuit, but your body, shoes, and the floor would allow the electricity to move through you.

If you were to touch another conductive object at the same time, though—ideally, in this case, wet lips to mic grill—then *zappola*.

I used my cell-phone flashlight to locate the tool kit's small Phillips head screwdriver, unscrewed the cable's silver cap, and slid it forward, exposing three wires: positive, negative and ground. I wiggled the ground free from its connection. As often as John let the mic drop, no one would even wonder about the loose wire. I reassembled the cable, wiping up behind me with the make-up remover pad just in case anyone *did* get suspicious.

Back indoors, I tiptoed down the hotel hallway. A door flew open, and there was John, his chest and feet now bare.

"What are you doing?" he said.

I swallowed. Did he have some inkling what I'd been up to?

He poked a finger at my chest. "You're charged up, like when you wrote 'Maybe.'"

I almost laughed with relief.

"No kidding, are you writing a song?"

"Yup," I said. "It's electrifying."

"What's it called? And don't give me that 'Midnight Oil in Fresno' crap."

"It's called 'Lights Out.'"

"Great title."

My resolve wobbled.

Then he stepped forward, lips coming in for a landing. I planted both hands on his chest and shoved. "What about Carmelita?"

"Ah, Carmelita," he said sadly, looking down in a way that seemed pensive, as though he were considering whether to tell me something. "She's not you, babe," he said at last. "She lacks your—music."

I shook my head, although there was truth to John's words. Carmelita was a beauty, but she couldn't even carry a tune.

"I'm writing something, too," he said.

I stopped and turned, crossing my arms over my chest. "Right. What's it called?"

"'Perhaps.'"

"'Perhaps'? So you're ripping me off *again*?"

"Shh."

"Oh, my God. You're *shushing* me?" I burned with indignation.

"Sorry," he said. "I've had a few."

"Save it for Carmelita." I held my key card to the door. The lock winked its green light.

"You know, Carmelita and—"

I slammed the door in his face.

Over the next few weeks, I experienced many moments when I considered reattaching the ground wire in the microphone cable—and many others when I tingled with anticipation as Michael plugged in the adapter. I had no idea what was going on with Carmelita; she had not returned my last two "just checking in" texts.

Our annual gig at the Salinas Valley Fair was in September. The portable outdoor stage had a partial awning to protect us from the Indian summer sun and the brutal reflection from the stage's springy, lightweight metal. I climbed down the back steps to find a power source. As usual, the venue was chaotic, with extension cords snaked here and there over a bare strip of earth and in through the open window of a fairgrounds building.

John's adapter was already plugged into an extension. *Sweet.*

Michael pointed me toward a heavy-duty but ancient drop cord, where he'd connected a box with four outlets, a couple of them already taken. "Use that."

Above us, Fred picked his way through the bass line that had been haunting me ever since I'd overheard it in Fresno. "What's that?" I asked Michael.

He waved his arms to shoo away two teenagers and sprang up the steps without answering my question.

I climbed up to my piano, grateful for the shade. My blouse was already sticking to my back.

For this gig, we'd ferried our own soundboard and speakers. Michael had joined John to make final adjustments.

When we got underway, a small but expectant crowd had gathered. We launched with our cover of "Friend of the Devil," which we extended into a true Dead jam with interspersed solos over verse chords—a comfortable way to get the party started. More people gathered—sleeveless tie-dye and bare feet and waving arms. My mood soared.

As we made our way through our first set, clouds scudded in. The day didn't get cooler, just more and more muggy, gathering around us the smells of corn on the cob and hot dogs.

Rain spattered the awning, but the crowd stayed, dancing with their palms and faces tilted up to catch the drops. Water sprinkled the front of the stage, where John pranced close to the audience, blowing kisses to lovelies.

As our first forty-five minutes drew to a close, John unhooked the mic with a dramatic flourish.

Expectation filled the rain-freshened air.

"This song," he said, "is for someone special."

What now? He's dedicating my song *to someone? It better be Carmelita.*

"We have *history*," John said. "Know what I mean?"

The crowd whistled and hooted.

John waited for them to quiet. "No, this gal gave us—Dire Wolf—our best song."

He's dedicating my song to me?

He turned and swept his arm toward me. "It's time I repaid Carrie Cunningham, our fantastic keyboard player, for our biggest hit, 'Maybe.'"

The sultry heat was melting my knees into rubber. I gave the crowd a homecoming-queen wave.

John covered the mic and said, "A-minor, babe." Then he spun back to the audience. "So I bring you"—he swept a pointing finger over the crowd—"for the first time on stage, our new original, 'Peeeerrhaaps.'"

On bass, Fred plucked the insistent groove I'd heard earlier. The band snuck in.

Under his tight T-shirt, John's torso expanded with drawn breath, ready to belt out the lyrics.

I held my breath in anticipation.

The fingers of his right hand resting on his guitar strings, the mic clutched in his left, he sang, "Perhaps while in Fennario, if I'd been a better man..."

My eyes blurred with tears. We'd named my apartment after the place in the Dead's song.

John stepped forward into a trickle of water.

He slammed another power chord, and his lips kissed the mic.

He jolted backward and fell, taking the mic with him. The cable yanked the stand clattering onto the metal stage.

Music turned into stunned silence.

Michael leapt forward, booting John in the ribs. The mic bounced off his chest, popping across the stage. Michael kicked his arm away from his guitar strings.

"I'm a doctor!" A man scrambled up the back steps and ran past me, shouting, "Call 911."

Fred and Riley had their phones out before I could move.

Michael bounded down the back steps. "Don't touch anything until I disconnect the power!"

As the EMTs strapped John to a gurney, one of them said, "That kick to his chest probably saved his life—jumpstarted his heart."

Michael tucked his chin. "I was just trying to knock away the mic." He strode back to where I was packing my keyboard and held out John's charred XLR cable. "Jesus, Carrie," he whispered fiercely, "I know you went into my toolbox. What the fuck were you *thinking*?"

Hands shaking, I folded my piano stand.

He coiled a drop cord. "John's an asshole, but you didn't have to try to *kill* him."

"He's cheating on Carmelita," I croaked.

He snorted. "Carmelita moved out three months ago. Before Fresno."

I gasped. "She never told me."

"Too embarrassed, I imagine," Michael said. "Didn't want to hear 'I told you so.'" He placed his Stratocaster in its case as though putting a baby down for a nap.

"I wouldn't have said that."

"She would have heard it."

"So"—I hesitated—"so John's messing around was a reaction to the break-up?"

Michael snapped the case shut. "I'm not defending him. He's a womanizer, and he screwed you on the money."

I stepped toward my amp and stubbed my toe on my keyboard bag. I told myself to get my head in the game, but my mind was spinning, recalibrating reality.

"That new tune," Michael said, brushing a finger across his lip, "is going to be a hit." He disconnected the cable from my amp and wound it expertly. "Because of John."

I got the inference. I might have written "Maybe," but it was John who propelled it to greatness. I'd never be out front of a band. Tucked in the back of Dire Wolf was where I belonged.

Michael slammed the coiled cable against my chest. "And he wrote it for you."

Now don't jump to conclusions. John and I did not get back together, like the characters in some insipid romcom. We're in a band together, which is much more intimate.

Like I said, I had plenty of reasons to kill him.
But I didn't, and John lives to rock on.

American Beauty
Released November 1970

"Box of Rain"
"Friend of the Devil"
"Sugar Magnolia"
"Operator"
"Candyman"
"Ripple"
"Brokedown Palace"
"Till the Morning Comes"
"Attics of My Life"
"Truckin'"

"Box of Rain" is by Phil Lesh and Robert Hunter.
"Friend of the Devil" is by Jerry Garcia, John Dawson, and Hunter.
"Sugar Magnolia" is by Bob Weir and Hunter.
"Operator" is by Ron McKernan.
"Truckin'" is by Garcia, Lesh, Weir, and Hunter.
All other songs are by Garcia and Hunter.

FRIEND OF THE DEVIL
Josh Pachter

Back when Graham first offered me the gig, he warned me there were two absolute rules: no moving violations and no hitchhikers.

I could understand the "no tickets" thing: given the cargo he'd be paying me to haul from L.A. to San Francisco two or three times a month, the last thing either one of us needed would be some Smokie pulling me over for speeding or whatever on I-5 and making me open up the back of the eighteen-wheeler.

But no hitchhikers? What was he afraid of, that I'd pick up some hot-bodied chippie who turned out to be a hot-headed CHiPs in plainclothes?

Bottom line, Graham was an asshole back then and still is, imposing rules because he *can*, whether they make any sense or not, and I'd like nothing better than to tell him to fuck the fuck off.

Thing of it is, if I ever *do* get bear bit, he'll surely hear about it, since he owns the rig. And he's the asshole who pays me, so I can't cuss him out to his ugly face. Which means the only way I have of saying "Fuck you, Graham" is by picking up the occasional thumber.

Which, this afternoon, I did.

Graham's call woke me a little after seven. My wife Mickey pulled her pillow over her head and groaned. "Jesus, Phil, it's *Sunday*."

But Graham doesn't give a rat's ass about weekends. When he has a shipment that has to move, I move it. So I stumbled out of bed and grabbed a quick shower, threw on some clothes and snatched my keys from the tray on my dresser, pulled the pillow down far enough to plant a kiss on Mickey's forehead, looked in on the baby to make sure he was sleeping, and headed out.

By the time I got to the lot in Eastvale and Graham's grunts had the truck loaded and ready to roll, it was almost noon. I buckled myself in and took off, and as I merged off the cloverleaf onto the 71 northbound, I tipped my Chino Cowboys ball cap to the California Institution for Men, just visible to the east. Almost a decade ago, I did four months of a six-month bid for shoplifting there before they sprang me for good behavior. I was nineteen, and that was my first and only conviction, but you have no idea how hard it is for an ex-con to find a decent job, which is why I was still driving for Graham at twenty-eight. His application process was pretty simple—"You lookin' for work, there, sport?"—and he even paid my way through truck school to get me my CDL.

It's an eight-hour run from Chino to San Fran, a little over four hundred miles. The semi's tank holds three hundred gallons, and at about six and a half miles to the gallon I can make the round trip four times without stopping to refuel. That afternoon, though, I pulled off the highway to top off at the Fill-More outside Bakersfield as usual. They've got the best price on diesel up and down Highway 5, but I'd stop there even if they didn't, because of the name.

My name, see, is Philip Moore. Phil Moore, get it? As in Fill-More?

Anyway, I refilled my tank and grabbed a coffee and was hoisting myself back into the cab when a polite voice below me said, "Excuse me, sir?"

Maybe it was the "sir?" that stopped me. I am not used to being sir'd.

The kid looked to be in his teens, surely no older than twenty or twenty-one. His jeans were worn white at the knees but not shotgunned like they buy them nowadays at H&M and Uniqlo, and he had on the first Western shirt with imitation-pearl snaps I've seen in a while. A white straw cowboy hat and a dusty pair of boots I was pretty sure were Tecovas and must have set him or his parents back at least two or three hundred bucks completed the ensemble. Out of keeping with the rest of his Wild West attire, he had a brand-new Fjällräven Kånken backpack slung over his shoulder.

"If you're heading north," he said politely, "I'd sure appreciate it if you'd let me ride with you a while."

Fuck you, Graham, I thought.

I had Channel 29 on the SiriusXM, and the kid sat beside me in the cab, his arms wrapped around the backpack on his lap, bobbing back and forth to "Chalkdust Torture."

"How far you going?" he asked over the music.

"Baghdad on the Bay," I said. "AKA San Francisco. Where *you* headed?"

"Reno. My sister lives up that way."

"Reno's a nice town." I jutted out my lower lip and nodded. "I might make it up there myself in a couple of days. Once I drop my load in San Fran, I'm gonna spend some time with my wife Donna in Cherokee, 'bout an hour and a half north of Sac'to. Then, if she can stand to be without me for a while, I'd love to run over to Reno and play a little blackjack there at the Grand Sierra. You know the Grand Sierra?"

"Biggest casino in town." He smiled shyly. "I'm a year away from old enough for the tables, but I've been known to slip the odd quarter into a slot."

We rode along in companionable silence for a bit, and then the kid stirred and said, "You start out in Bakersfield this morning?"

"Nope. I been with my wife Mickey in Chino the last week."

His brow furrowed beneath the brim of his hat. "Your wife Mickey? I thought you were on your way to see your wife Donna?"

I grinned. "You know what they say, son: man's got himself two wives, that's bigamy—but he's got him only got *one* wife, why, that's monotony."

He laughed at that, but I could see out of the corner of my eye that the joke had made him uncomfortable.

"Do they know about each other?" he said after a while. "Your two wives, I mean."

I snorted. "I may be dumb," I replied, "but I'm not *stupid.* I spend two or three nights a week with each of 'em, most weeks, and as far as they're concerned, I'm on the road the rest of the time."

He nodded, processing the information. And then, apparently interested, he asked a follow-up. "You figure two's enough? Ever consider adding any more to your string?"

I reached for the dash and turned down the music. Left it playing, but brought the volume down so I didn't have to fight it. "You remember what I said about the Grand Sierra? Well, truth be told, it's not just the blackjack that draws me. Couple months ago, I got to talking to one of the dealers, and, man, she is *sweet.* Anne Marie, her name is. We've gotten pretty hot and heavy, and sure, I could see making her Wife Number Three, somewhere along the line. Indeed, I could."

My hands were on the wheel—ten and two, nice and safe with thirty tons of eighteen-wheeler and cargo behind me—and he raised his chin at them and asked, "This dealer, she hasn't spotted your ring?"

I shook my head. "You think I wear a wedding ring into the casino, son? I already told you, I'm not *stupid.*"

He subsided into silence.

"Can I bum a cigarette?" he said, after we'd burned through another couple of miles and were coming up on the exit for Kettleman City. "I should've bought some back at the truck stop, but I didn't think of it."

"Sorry," I said, "I don't smoke."

Which was ironic, given I was buttlegging ten master cases of counterfeit Marlboros in the back of the rig. Another one of Graham's mules had smuggled them across the Mexican border, and there'd be a crew ready to unload them when I hit San Francisco.

Let me do the math here: a master case consists of fifty cartons, a carton holds ten packs, and a pack contains the usual twenty sticks and boasts a fake tax stamp. So I had eighty *thousand* imitation Marlboros on me, but not a one I could hand over to my passenger.

Like I said, ironic.

I'm not a member of Graham's inner circle, so I don't know the exact numbers, but I figure he probably buys the merch for like fifty cents a pack. A pack of Marlboros costs upwards of ten bucks in California, so my guess is Graham sells them to a distributor for five. The distributor moves them for maybe eight and almost doubles his money, while Graham—the enterprise's mastermind—multiplies his original investment ten times over, less what he pays me and the rest of the chain. He's *got* to be clearing at least two or three dollars a pack, so the load I was carrying—lemme see, ten master cases times fifty cartons each is five hundred cartons, times ten packs per carton is five thousand packs, times two or three bucks' profit per pack is ten to fifteen grand per run. Sheesh. And the mastermind doesn't even get his hands dirty.

Graham's ripping off both the folks who make the *real* Marlboros and the taxman, so I guess that makes him something of a devil. Tell you the truth, though, I'd rather be the devil's friend than his enemy...

Anyway, I turned Phish back up loud, and we rode on for another two hours through the heart of central California. It was around six thirty in the afternoon, as we were nearing Santa Nella, that the kid seemed to come to a decision about something.

He unzipped his backpack and reached inside it and came out holding a single-action pistol with a white pearl grip. I have no idea what make or model gun it was, but he was pointing it at my face and it looked perfectly capable of blowing my brains out the other side of my head.

"Whoa, there, partner," I said. "What the *fuck* are you doing?"

He leaned forward and switched off the radio with his free hand.

"What *you're* doing," he said, "is getting off at this exit and heading west on 152."

"For *what*?"

"For staying alive." He cocked the hammer. "You read me?"

I read him. The gun in his hand was pretty damn legible.

So I got off the highway and headed west on 152. We threaded the needle between the San Luis Reservoir and the O'Neill Forebay and then looped around southwest onto the Pacheco Pass Highway. Just past Mysterious Mountaintop, he had me pull into the Bell Station Farmers Market, which was closed and deserted except for one dark-green Kia Soul at the far end of the row of parking spaces. It had to be my imagination, since we were still half an hour east of Gilroy, but I could almost smell the garlic wafting our way.

"What's this all about?" I demanded.

Okay, fine, "demanded" is an exaggeration. I wasn't in any position to demand a damn thing. What I did was *ask*, and in all honesty *plead* might be a bit closer to the truth. I mean, I had a cocked pistol about eighteen inches from the side of my head.

"Turn off the engine," he ordered me.

"I usually let it run for five minutes," I said, "let it cool down a—"

"Turn it off," he repeated.

I turned it off.

"Now get out of the truck," he said.

"Are you hijacking me?"

"Get out of the truck," he said again, his tone exactly the same.

I did what he told me, and he squeezed past the wheel and came down right behind me.

With the barrel of his weapon poking my ribs, he pushed me around to the back of the trailer.

"Open it up," he commanded.

Man, the kid must have *really* wanted a smoke. Except how did he know what I was carrying? I sure as hell hadn't told him.

I unlocked the padlock and opened the swing doors.

And then the driver's door of that green Kia swung open, and a figure stepped out of the car.

A woman. Tall, slender. Long blond hair tied back in a ponytail. Dressed in a pair of cutoff denim shorts and a tight yellow tank top.

She walked toward us, her features washed out by the late-afternoon sunlight. It wasn't until she was less than a dozen feet away that I saw who she was.

"Anne Marie?" I said, hardly believing it. "What are you—?"

"Check out his ring finger, sis," the kid said.

"So he *is* married." She sighed. "Goddamn it, I *thought* so."

"Twice," the kid added.

"What happened to the first one? Divorced, or did she—?"

"No, twice *now*. He's got a wife down by L.A., and another one up north of Sacramento someplace I never heard of."

"Really?" She shook her head. "Oh, Philip, I knew you were a liar, but *this* truly takes me by surprise."

"Honey," I said, "I can explain."

"You been watching too much TV," Little Brother growled. "There's no explanation that'll get you out of this, *Philip.* Cell phone, please."

"But I—"

"*Cell phone,*" he barked.

I took it out of my pocket and handed it over.

"Now up and in," he said.

I climbed up into the back of the trailer and turned to look down at them.

"Are you going to shoot me?"

"Shoot you?" said Anne Marie sweetly. "No, Philip, of course not. That would be murder. We're just going to leave you here to consider the error of your ways. My original idea was to let your wife know where you are, so she could send someone to release you. But now..."

Her voice trailed off.

"But now?" I said, and by this point I was on my knees, tears welling up in my eyes.

"But now," she went on, "why, I wouldn't know which wife to call."

"Call them both!" I screamed as the kid swung the doors shut and I heard the padlock snick into place. "I'll give you the numbers, Anne Marie! For the love of God, call them both!"

There was no response. A minute later, I heard the faint rumble of Anne Marie's Soul starting up and taking off, and after that there was nothing but silence.

Little Brother heard me say Mickey's and Donna's names, and both their numbers are in my contacts. Maybe Anne Marie or the kid will call one of 'em, after all. Or they could just put in an anonymous call to the cops.

Or, shit, they could call Mickey *and* Donna and bust me to both of them. *That* would fuck me over but good.

I doubt they'll lift a finger to help me, though. I know who they are, and them locking me up like this has got to be at least six different kinds of felony.

Nope, I'm afraid I'm stuck.

I've got nothing to eat or drink, and I have no idea when the Farmer's Market opens for business. Today's Sunday. If they're closed through next Saturday, I'm probably a dead man. If they operate every day, though, I ought to be able to survive one night in this tin can.

And then what? Ring the cops and tell 'em what happened?

It'd be Anne Marie and her brother's word against mine, and I expect they've both probably arranged themselves an alibi for the day. Plus, if I bring the law into this, I can guaranteed kiss my gig with Graham goodbye. Last thing he wants is that kind of attention from the Man.

So here I sit, in the dark, surrounded by cigarettes I couldn't smoke even if I wanted to, since I don't have a lighter or matches.

By touch, I rip open one of the master cases, rip open a dozen cartons and a hundred packs and arrange a couple thousand phony Marlboros in the shape of a mattress. It's no Sealy Posturepedic, but it'll be a shit-ton more comfortable than lying on the trailer's corrugated metal floor.

I lie down, hump cigarettes into the shape of a pillow, and try to relax.

I have no idea if I'll ever see daylight again, but I just might get some sleep tonight.

Grateful Dead (Skull & Roses)
Released September 1971

"**Bertha**"
"Mama Tried"
"Big Railroad Blues"
"Playing in the Band"
"The Other One"
"Me and My Uncle"
"Big Boss Man"
"Me and Bobby McGee"
"Johnny B. Goode"
"Wharf Rat"
"Not Fade Away/Goin' Down the Road Feeling Bad"

"Bertha" and "Wharf Rat" are by Jerry Garcia and Robert Hunter.
"Mama Tried" is by Merle Haggard.
"Big Railroad Blues" is by Noah Lewis.
"Playing in the Band" is by Bob Weir and Hunter.
"The Other One" is by Weir and Bill Kreutzmann.
"Me and My Uncle" is by John Phillips.
"Big Boss Man" is by Luther Dixon and Al Smith.
"Me and Bobby McGee" is by Fred Foster and Kris Kristofferson.
"Johnny B. Goode" is by Chuck Berry.
"Not Fade Away" is by Buddy Holly and Norman Petty.
"Goin' Down the Road Feeling Bad" is traditional.

BERTHA
Twist Phelan

Be worried the plastic cuff where it chafed her wrist. It'd been easier to get out of the building than out of the stupid bracelet. She used her fingernail to scratch off the last four letters of her first name: RTHA. Apparently her mother hadn't thought life would be hard enough already.

She'd settled on Be—one e, never two—after her transfer to the second—third?—high school. According to the dictionary, *be* was a verb "used to say something about a person, thing, or state, to show a permanent or temporary quality." Be liked that, especially the permanent or temporary part. Like Dr. Hunter had told her, there were some things she *was* and there were some things she *did*, and they weren't necessarily the same, though Be had found some people would disagree.

There was that play, too, the one from English class. *To be, or not to be, that is the question.* The teacher said the character was deciding whether to live or not live. Be got it. She wondered pretty much the same thing every day—should she be Be, or should she not be Be. That was her motherfrickin' question.

Be had left last night just after lights out, soft-padding her way through the big building's dark corridors and blind corners until she was outside, sprinting past Dr. Hunter's window, running, running, running until the houses became sparser, the area between them bigger, feet slapping down over and over until her side burned and there was no more pavement or streetlights, until the rain finally forced her to take shelter in an empty chicken coop beside a single-wide trailer all by its lonesome.

The drops pelting the tin roof made the best sound—*p-tat, p-tat, p-tat.* This helped her sleep, for once not dreaming. Or nightmaring. Nope, not one thought about the wrong things she'd done. Be had told Dr. Hunter sometimes doing the wrong thing was the only thing that felt right. Like if someone came at her or was thinking about coming at her or might someday come at her, she *had* to push back. She was a fighter, not a runner. At least until now. And she wasn't so much running from a place as from herself, her old self. No, Be was running toward the new Be, the one who didn't want to fight anymore.

Be woke just as the sky was starting to bruise, white-yellow and lavender flaring against faded denim blue. She changed into the army-green T-shirt and cargo pants she'd snagged from the clothesline behind the trailer and took a swig from a plastic bottle filled from the water tank beside it. Nibbling on the granola bar saved from yesterday's lunch, she jogged back to the fire road, the rainwater in its ruts a muddy golden color, a strange tea made of desert clay.

Her mother's fourth—fifth?—boyfriend believed in karma. He'd told Be the universe was keeping a record of everything good and everything bad she did, and how she acted in this life determined what or who she'd come back as in her next life.

"If you're good, you come back as somebody beautiful, or rich, or famous," he said. "If you're bad, you're reincarnated as a bug or something."

Be thought it might not be too awful to be a bug—hanging out in the grass all day, keeping to herself, doing bug stuff. But she hadn't said anything.

Most of the people Be grew up around believed the circumstances they'd been born into and anything positive and negative that came into their lives were all a product of divine chance, emphasis on *divine*. Whether or not you were beautiful or successful in business or lucky in love was decided by a god. Make that the God.

Be preferred the possibility that her actions in a prior life were dictating her fate, that she deserved the life she was leading. Every step she'd taken as whoever she'd been before had led to who she was right now.

"There aren't no menus at the karma cafe," her mother's boyfriend used to say. "You're served what you deserve."

A new thought pushed into her brain mid-stride and she faltered, nearly tripped. Was being Be a step up or a step down? Could this go-round possibly be an improvement from what came before? She suppressed a shudder.

Be had done some bad things, things that made even her mother not want her to come around anymore. But Dr. Hunter said she was more than the most awful thing she'd ever done. He'd also told Be it was up to her who she wanted to be.

"It's never too late for a fresh start, Bertha."

Bertha...Birth...Rebirth...Re-Bertha. Maybe next time she'd call herself ReBe.

Could she really begin again? Reincarnate herself without dying first? Or did Dr. Hunter mean she could be good enough so next time she'd come back as a...what? Movie star? Gnat?

Maybe she'd change her name right now. *ReBe. ReBe. ReBe.* Stuff got stuck on endless loops in her brain. Sometimes it was soothing. Sometimes it was annoying.

Hours passed, motionless desert yawning empty around her, as she trudged along the dirt track. Shadows lost their noonday edges and pushed out from under bushes, claiming territory. Now and then Be squinted at the horizon, where pomegranate-tinted hills that had looked attainable kept their distance, barely changing perspective as she walked toward them. Beyond them was the ocean.

She'd thought this would be easier. A crow swooped low and settled on an ocotillo beside the track. As though reading her thoughts, it chuckled derisively.

Be stared into the bird's pitiless eyes, wondering what or who it had been before. Was being a crow a promotion or a demotion? Did you have to work your way up gradually, each existence a little bit better than the prior, or was it possible to be so good, so blazingly worthy that you catapulted from bug to human, from Be to ReBe?

That was why she'd run. She was ready to be reincarnated now. Part of her new start meant leaving the parched earth and air she'd always known for the ocean's rejuvenating waters. *Rejuvenate. ReBe.* She closed her eyes and imagined walking into the sea, dropping to her knees in the salty froth, feeling the tug and push of the tide.

An engine cleared its throat in the distance behind her. Be puffed out a small sigh.

She could dart for cover. Or she could wait for the engine to rumble up next to her, the door to screech open, the feet to thud on the sunburned dirt.

To be Be or not to be Be.

"Hey," a voice called. "You okay?"

Be opened her eyes. "Yeah."

A pickup truck was stopped beside her. It was the first vehicle Be had seen since she turned onto the fire road four hours ago.

The driver, a man in his forties wearing a faded T-shirt and a trucker cap decorated with a skull wearing a crown of red roses, was looking at her over the hood.

"You sure you're okay, miss?"

"I'm fine," Be said. As the familiar helplessness washed over her, she had the sense she was falling, falling, falling...

Dr. Hunter had talked to her about it. She knew what he'd say if he could see her now. *Bertha, you have a choice—*

"Where're you going? Next town is ten miles away and there's nothing between here and there." The man walked around the truck's front. "It's not safe being out here by yourself."

Be edged backward. "It's okay. I'm fine." A bird floated past, high overhead. The crow she'd seen earlier? Be had never felt so isolated.

The man moved closer. He had a face made to be cheerful, with friendly brown eyes crinkled at the corners and a mouth used to smiling. "You're not even wearing real shoes."

Be glanced down at the rubber shower slides. The toes of her socks were red with clay.

"I have a daughter about your age," the man said. "I wouldn't feel right leaving a young lady out here on her lonesome."

Be's heart beat hard and high in her chest. "I'm good, thanks."

"Tell you what. You can ride in the cab or even the truck bed, if you want. I'll keep the doors unlocked and the windows down."

"No, really, I don't—" Be stopped, hearing the quaver in her voice. He probably did, too. She licked her lips, tasting dust. "I don't want to trouble you."

The man reached into the pocket of khakis the Gap had last sold ten years ago, pulled out a phone, and held it up. "As soon as we're back in range you can call whoever you want. Or, if you really want to stay here, you can give me a number and I'll call it and ask them to come get you." He spread his hands. Be noticed his nails were clean and trimmed short, like Dr. Hunter's. "Whatever you want."

Be thought about it. Maybe this was the fresh start Dr. Hunter had talked about. Maybe this was her opportunity to move up the karmic ladder.

"A ride would be good, thanks," she said.

The man reached for the door handle, making Be jump. He opened the door wide and stood, waiting.

Heart pumping with hope, Be clambered awkwardly into the seat. After a moment's consideration, she wedged the bag carrying her clothes and other stuff into the space between her seat and the console. Dr. Hunter's voice, questions from their sessions, began to loop through her head.

Bertha, why did you skip group therapy? Bertha, why didn't you take your meds? Bertha, why aren't you sleeping?

Because I was being Be was all she could ever think to say. The man slammed the door beside her, jolting her out of her thoughts. She watched him walk around the front of the truck and climb in beside her.

He started the truck and lowered the windows. "This okay?"

Be nodded.

"Let me know if you get too cold and I'll put the heat on." The man put the truck in gear.

"Okay." Be thought about being the new Be. "Thank you," she said, feeling her shoulders unclench.

"How 'bout some tunes?"

The man tapped the dashboard screen. A cacophony of rock, blues, and country burst forth, reminding Be of the jam sessions the karma-believing boyfriend listened to when he smoked weed and claimed one of his prior selves had been at Woodstock.

As the truck started moving, Be listened to the music, trying to find the melody.

"I'm Ron, by the way. What's your name?" the man said.

Be touched her bag of things, then pulled her hand away. She felt her chest expand, fill with possibility. "ReBe."

"Reba? Like the singer? That's nice." He reached out and patted her thigh.

And left his hand there.

"You're nice, too, aren't you?" he said.

Hope drained from Be like water from a cracked glass. So much for choices. She pulled her bag onto her lap and hugged it, rocking slightly.

A moment later, Phil wrenched the wheel hard to the right. Be screamed, a thin primal cry, and grabbed the handle over the door to stop herself from being thrown forward.

The truck lurched left, then rolled forward another few yards and stopped. Phil lay slumped over the wheel.

Be pushed the gear shift into park, scrambled out, ran around to the driver's door, and opened it. She grasped Phil's upper arm and tugged hard.

He spilled onto the dirt road and lay there, motionless. Be stepped over the body and got behind the wheel. The ocean had just gotten a whole lot closer.

There was blood on the knife she'd stolen from the kitchen. She wiped the blade clean on the seat, then used it to slice through her hospital ID bracelet. As she flicked the strip of plastic out the window, Dr. Hunter's voice returned.

Bertha, is this who you really want to be?

An upward flutter of dark wings caught her eye through the windshield.

What good was being reincarnated, she thought as she drove away, *if you just came back as who you were before?*

Wake of the Flood
Released October 1973

"Mississippi Half-Step Uptown Toodeloo"
"Let Me Sing Your Blues Away"
"Row Jimmy"
"Stella Blue"
"Here Comes Sunshine"
"Eyes of the World"
"Weather Report Suite: Prelude, Part I, Part II (Let It Grow)"

"Let Me Sing Your Blues Away" is by
Keith Godchaux and Robert Hunter.
"Weather Report Suite" is by Bob Weir,
Eric Andersen, and John Perry Barlow.
All other songs are by Jerry Garcia and Hunter.

EYES OF THE WORLD
K.L. Murphy

Clara Borges' head rolled toward the flickering light of the screen. A woman with hair that fell to her waist and snow-white teeth talked, as images of the Met Gala appeared one after another behind her. As Clara watched, the camera zoomed in on a man in a suit made entirely of shimmering boas. The outfit was outrageous, which she supposed was the idea. She remembered her own evenings at the Met, her own gowns, and wondered when the world had shifted to a place where boa suits and recycled plastic dresses counted as fashion.

With a heavy sigh, she closed her eyes, sinking deeper into the pillow. It was the sound of her own name that snapped her awake.

"What a career Clara Borges has had." A man in a coat and jeans joined the woman on the screen.

With a shaky hand, Clara reached out and turned up the volume.

"You're so right," the toothy woman said.

"As you know, Elena, Ms. Borges won an Oscar for the feminist thriller *And Woman*. She was nominated twice more—once for *Happiness, My Darling* and again for *This Way to Calcutta*—but it was her role as Leeza in *And Woman* that made her a household name."

Elena nodded. "That's right, John Lee, and she won a Golden Globe ten years ago when she played Shelly Hunt's mother in *Me and Mine.* Bu-ut," she said with a wag of her finger, "we both know movies aren't the only thing Clara Borges is famous for. Don't forget all those marriages and divorces."

John Lee chuckled, although Clara didn't think there was anything funny about it. "I've heard it said that the heart has its seasons, but Clara Borges's love life has had more seasons than most."

"Too true. And who could forget the Oprah interview? That story about growing up homeless, living in a car for years? I mean, talk about the American dream."

"Yep. No doubt about it, she was quite a woman."

"You'd think I was dead," Clara muttered, pushing herself up on her elbows.

From the corner of the screen, her own face stared back at her, making her wince. She didn't look *bad,* not exactly—not for seventy-eight, anyway. She could easily pass for seventy, even sixty-five, with none of the stretched skin that made her peers look like hairless cats. Still, no matter how exceptional her plastic surgeon was, he couldn't turn back time. Never again would she be the thirty-five-year-old who'd won that golden statue or the ingenue who'd starred opposite Robert Houseman, her husband three times over. Nor the woman who'd eloped after a twenty-one-day courtship with a man ten years her junior. Surprisingly, that marriage had lasted a decade. And then there was Tony, her final husband, who died before she could divorce him, the tricky bastard.

"Sources say that Ms. Borges is suffering from an undisclosed illness," the man said, face grim now. "We've heard that the legendary actress may not make it through the week."

Clara's fingers curled around her satin bedsheet. "Lies."

"What lies?" Allie, Clara's assistant, spoke over the theme music, as the show cut to a new story.

Clara pointed a bony finger at the television. "They say I'm dying."

"Oh." Allie picked up the remote, and the screen went black.

"That's all you have to say? 'Oh'?"

With a sigh, the girl faced Clara. "Well, *everyone* dies, sooner or later, Ms. Borges, so it's not really a lie."

Clara's mouth puckered. "Don't be facetious." Why were all of her assistants so worthless? Allie had been there less than three months and was already proving to be a disappointment. Sadly, Clara couldn't afford to lose another one so soon. "They're saying I won't survive the week, and *that's* a bald-faced lie."

Silent this time, Allie stared at her with that weird, watchful gaze, the one that always reminded Clara of a little brown bird.

"Never mind. Bring me my robe, will you?"

The girl sprang into action, helping Clara into her dressing gown and escorting her to the sitting room. Allie clicked another remote, and a whirring sounded as the blinds rose high to reveal floor-to-ceiling windows and a view of the Pacific Ocean. Whitecaps bobbed on the horizon like floating marshmallows, and seagulls circled nearby. Clara's third husband had said the house was too high up on the cliff, restricting access to the sea, but she'd liked it for that very reason. She loved to watch the ocean from above, the way the color of the water changed with the wind, the way the waves crashed against the rocks. The ocean had a power that couldn't be contained, like her.

"Can you get my publicist on the phone?" she asked, thinking of the horrid news report.

The girl shot her another one of those odd looks. "I would, but you fired her last month, Ms. Borges."

"Of course I did. She was an imbecile." Clara's answer came automatically, like a reflex, and she racked her brain, trying to remember the publicist's name. Sometimes, memories flew away faster than she could catch them.

"I've been taking care of the correspondence, Ms. Borges," Allie said. She summarized the most recent emails, one of which proposed a documentary on the making of *And Woman*, but Clara lost track of the words, struck by a sense of déjà vu. The sensation wasn't altogether unpleasant, but wholly unlike any she'd known before. It wasn't the scene or the conversation that felt familiar. Quite the opposite. The focus of the strange feeling had nothing to do with her and everything to do with Allie.

Unable to make sense of it, Clara studied the girl from under her lashes. Allie moved with a lightness and grace Clara hadn't noticed before. She thought the girl's face was unremarkable, but she liked her long, elegant hands and the dark hair that shimmered in soft waves. Clara had always wanted hair like that, but instead she'd had stick-straight hair that needed extensions and color to add dimension, all part of her Hollywood transformation. None of that explained the feeling, though. Perhaps the girl reminded her of someone? Another assistant—or, God help her, the publicist?

"Your editor wants to know when you're going to finish the manuscript," Allie said, bringing Clara back from her musings.

The manuscript. Her memoir had been three years in the making, and she still wasn't finished. How could she conclude the story of her life when she wasn't done living it?

"What should I tell him, Ms. Borges?"

Clara pulled her dressing gown tight, her thin lips pressed into a hard line. She didn't want to talk about the damn book. "Tell me, Allie, what did you want to be when you grew up?"

The girl blinked like a stupid animal, and Clara groaned. Now she would think she cared.

"Well," Allie said, finally finding her voice, "I guess I wanted to be a dancer. I took ballet for years and was in a regional company for a while, but the truth is, I wasn't good enough."

Well, that explained the perfect posture. "And then?"

The girl was silent so long that Clara's mind wandered. Dancers had horrible feet. She'd seen that for herself on the set of *And Woman*. One of the characters, a retired dancer, was played by an actual ballerina. After seeing the discolored nails, bunions, and raw skin on her heels, Clara couldn't understand why anyone would want to dance on their toes. Her gaze went to Allie's feet now, but they were sensibly covered in white sneakers. Thank heaven for small favors.

Belatedly, she remembered she'd asked the girl a question. "What did you say?"

Allie's cheeks flushed pink. "I said I hoped to be discovered."

"I see." The older woman couldn't hide her annoyance. "An actress, then."

The girl flinched as though Clara had struck her. What had she expected? This town was filled with girls like Allie, pretty enough, but ultimately lacking the two essential things a woman needed to succeed. It didn't take beauty, a quick wit, or even talent. It took ruthlessness and sacrifice. Clara had stepped over former friends and jilted lovers, had given up the idea of having a family—all in the name of stardom. And it had paid off. She'd won the awards. She'd graced the cover of every magazine. For decades, she'd had the eyes of the world upon her. Even in semi-seclusion, she was still news.

Cursing herself for opening the door, Clara braced for the inevitable request for advice or introduction, but to Allie's credit, none came. Instead, she said, "I can help you finish the book, if you'd like."

The book again. Although part of her wanted to be done with it, another part held back. During negotiations, the publisher had offered a ghost writer to speed up the process, but Clara had declined. Why would she want someone else to craft her story? It belonged to her. Except it didn't, did it? Once her memoir appeared in print, it would belong to everyone. Was that what she was afraid of?

The last months, it had been slow going. It took more effort to find the right words, and she tired quickly. Her brain, once as powerful as the ocean she loved, was dying, little by little. Hiding it was getting more difficult, but the truth was, if she didn't finish the damn book soon, she wouldn't be able to. Perhaps it wouldn't hurt to give the girl a chance.

***

Two hours later, Clara's brain buzzed with energy. Allie had a gentle way of encouraging her to talk, and the words flowed out of her as the girl typed. Maybe she *would* be able to finish the dratted book, after all.

Sitting back, the girl tucked loose strands of hair behind her ear in one smooth motion. Clara's heart skipped a beat. There it was again. That odd feeling. This time, it was the girl's mannerism, the delicate way her fingers moved. Clara's gaze moved from Allie's hands to her face. The nose was familiar, too, wasn't it? If only she could remember who it reminded her of.

"Ms. Borges, I noticed you skipped over chapter fifteen. Would you like to work on that after you rest?"

Clara's eyes narrowed. Why was the girl asking about chapter fifteen? Did she know something? But she dismissed the thought immediately. It was impossible. No one knew about it. Still, that albatross of a chapter wouldn't go away. She'd started it, but no matter how she tried, the words wouldn't come. The chapter would cover the year before she began filming *And Woman*. She still remembered getting the script, remembered the chills that crawled up her spine when she read it for the first time. She'd begged her agent to get her an audition. They didn't want her, of course, but she'd never let that stop her before.

Clara was a woman who did what needed to be done. She wasn't that way before her mother died, but later she learned how life really worked. She'd told the truth in that Oprah interview, not sugarcoating the image of a child sleeping in a broken-down Olds or scrounging for food with rats. But the things she left out were far worse. At twelve, she'd stabbed a man for a half-eaten loaf of bread. At thirteen, she'd learned to trade the only thing she had left for blankets and shoes. She wasn't ashamed, but she was smart enough to know the public wouldn't accept her as America's anything if they knew the truth.

She'd approached getting the part of Leeza as though her life depended on it, and maybe it had. Unfortunately, she hadn't taken adequate precautions. After years of starvation, her body's cycles had never been regular, and by the time she realized what had happened, it was too late. She'd been forced to hide away until the ordeal was over, no one the wiser.

In a stroke of luck, her short-term disappearing act "to prepare for the role" became fodder for her legend. Studios took her seriously. The public ate it up. At the time, she'd buried the truth—the same way she'd buried her past—but lately she'd been wondering. She'd never been a woman prone to self-reflection, but if she had any soul left, what did it think? It occurred to her that maybe she didn't want to know.

When Allie shook her awake, Clara struggled to recall her dreams. In one, she'd been a girl in a pink dress, carrying a stuffed rabbit and holding a woman's hand—but every time she tried to see the woman's face, the vision slipped away. Her mind cleared as she sipped a cup of tea, but she couldn't shake a feeling of sadness, as though she'd lost something precious.

"Where did you grow up, Allie?" Clara asked, as they settled into their seats. This must have been included in the girl's background check, but she doubted she'd paid attention.

"Kansas City. On the Kansas side."

Clara didn't really know or care what that meant, but she needed a few more minutes before diving back into the book. "Siblings?"

"A younger brother."

"I suppose you're close."

"Not really," the girl said, squirming a bit. "He's ten years younger, so I was gone a lot when he was growing up. He was a surprise baby, I think."

"Sounds nice, though." Clara didn't know why she'd said that. In fact, the girl's story sounded boring as hell.

"Yeah, I guess. But I like California a lot better. It doesn't snow here, for one thing."

"True, but there's the rain. I suppose you miss your family."

The girl bit her lip, and Clara wondered if she'd hit a nerve. Perhaps Allie was homesick, despite the warmer weather.

"My parents are good people," she said, "but they don't really understand me. I mean, I look exactly like my mom, and I love her, but we're nothing alike. She's like a tornado, with all these ideas and projects, but she never finishes any of them. One month she wants to paint, and the next she's into pottery, and then it's gardening or learning to make sushi. My dad always says how talented she is, but I don't know how you can tell. She doesn't stick with anything and—"

The girl stopped talking. "I'm sorry, Ms. Borges. You don't want to hear any of this."

Clara didn't, and yet she liked the sound of Allie's voice. "How are you different from your mother?"

"Do you really want to know?"

The frankness of the question surprised her, impressed her. "Yes, I think I do."

"Well, the obvious thing is that I finish what I start. I was four when I started taking ballet. I knew I was good, even then. My mother kept asking if I wanted to try jazz or hip-hop, but I never wavered. It was ballet or nothing." She paused to take a breath. "I took lessons all through high school. I was in *The Nutcracker* every year, and I joined a regional company the minute I graduated. I even got the lead a few times, but I couldn't take it any further. Not that I didn't try. I auditioned for three of the more prestigious companies, more times than I can count, but I just wasn't good enough. I was *good*, but I wasn't *great*, not the way you have to be." She cocked her head to one side. "For a long time, I kept going. Quitting wasn't an option, until I looked at it from a different perspective."

Clara lifted one eyebrow. "And what was that?"

"That it's not quitting if you've taken it as far as it can go. I'd ridden that train to the end of the line—for me, anyway. I would have liked to go further, but I figured that, if I didn't get off then, I might miss the next one."

"And being an actress was the next one?" Again, that vague disappointment in the girl. "That's what you want now?"

Surprising Clara a second time, Allie shook her head. "No, I don't think I'd be a very good actress."

"Well, that makes you unlike every other girl who's ever come to L.A. Why *did* you come out to California, then?"

"The ocean, for one thing."

Her words jolted a long-ago memory, and Clara shifted toward the window and the dark waves. Hadn't it been the promise of the ocean that had first drawn her away from the streets of Tucson? Day after day, she'd sat on the pilings, watched the water churn beneath her feet, and planned her future. She'd made a vow in front of the ocean, a promise to make something of herself. And she had.

"But I also came to meet someone," Allie added.

Clara's interest faded. Young girl looking for love. Blah, blah, blah.

"Someone I'd wanted to know my whole life but didn't know existed before."

Allie's arched tone got her attention again. "That sounds mysterious."

"Yeah, right? See, I'd been doing all this research on my family, and some of it didn't make sense. Did you know you can find out all this stuff on DNA and ancestry sites? Anyway, my mom got kinda pissed, so I stopped telling her what I was doing. That was my dad's idea."

"Why would your mother care?"

"She didn't want to hurt my grandparents' feelings. They adopted her when she was a baby, the year you were preparing for *And Woman*."

Adopted. Clara's stomach clenched, and she stared at the girl. Was that her mother's nose? No, it had to be a coincidence. Lots of people shared features and characteristics. It didn't mean anything. How many times had someone tried this sort of scam before?

Allie kept talking. "When I came here, I knew right away it would be a mistake to force the situation. What if you didn't like me? What if I didn't like you? So I decided to find a way to get to know you that wouldn't be a whole big scene, you know. And I really do love California. That's kind of a bonus."

"But you said you came here to be discovered," Clara said, her voice half-rebuke, half-question.

"Stupid, right? That first day, I was so nervous, wondering if you'd recognize me." She grimaced. "That shows how idiotic I am. I mean, they told me at the agency, *stay in the background, don't be intrusive.* How would you even notice me, much less discover I was your—"

The words fell away.

After a moment, she resumed, apparently changing the subject. "You fired your publicist because there was cheese on your sandwich. Cheese."

"I don't like cheese."

"Yeah, well, you were kind of a bitch about it."

In spite of everything, the girl *was* amusing. "It's not the first time someone's used that word to describe me."

"I figured. I almost packed up and went home after that."

"Thinking this train had also reached the end of the line?"

Allie smiled. "Almost. But I stayed because I noticed something else about you."

"And what was that?"

"You forget a lot."

Clara drew in a breath, her face hot.

"Nothing you can't play off or blame on someone else, but still. My grandmother—my dad's mom—has it, too." She hesitated. "I thought you seemed kind of lonely."

Embarrassment turned to indignation. "That's ridiculous."

The girl ignored her. "That's when I started thinking, maybe you don't know how to let anyone get close to you. I've read your bio, and I'm not stupid. Anyone who survived the streets for as long as you did has to be tough. I'm guessing trust was a luxury.

It explains why you couldn't stay married, right?"

Clara said nothing, her hands curled around the arms of the chair. This girl, whoever she was, had a nerve, presuming to know things about her. What did she want? Money?

"So I stayed, even though it's kind of a crappy job and the pay is terrible. I don't care about that, though. My dad sold this app the year my brother was born. He doesn't have to work anymore."

So maybe it *wasn't* about money.

"Sometimes it's not even really a job, though. Getting your bed ready, getting your tea, those are things I *like* doing for you, because, well, you know." She half-laughed. "That doesn't mean you aren't still a royal pain in the ass and there aren't times I want to strangle you. But I see how hard things are for you, like for my dad's mom."

A moment of silence stretched out between them. Did the girl see her as weak?

"You're tougher than her, though, way tougher. That's why I knew I couldn't blindside you. For one thing, you might call me crazy and throw me out, and I didn't want to lose you." The girl's cheeks grew pink. "And I wanted you to like me. At least a little."

Did she? Did she *like* Allie? Clara had never considered that before. Even if she did, she couldn't understand what the girl expected from her. Affirmation? Open arms? No. There had to be something else. She must be lying about the money.

"What do you want, Allie? Cash? A part? What?"

Eyes filling, the girl blinked, averting her face. By the time she stood up, back ramrod straight, any trace of tears was gone.

"I don't want anything, Ms. Borges. I'm sorry I bothered you. This"—she took a breath and waved a hand—"this never happened. I'll let the agency know you're looking for a replacement." With a nod, she backed away.

Clara's fingernails dug into the chair. Whatever she'd wanted from the girl, this wasn't it. "Wait."

Was Allie telling the truth? Or was she that great an actress?

Clara could find out, of course. There were tests for that sort of thing, but she realized she wanted very much to believe. She'd given up so much, done terrible things. Was it possible the universe was giving her one last chance at redemption before her memory faded away to nothing?

"Why?" Allie was looking at Clara, a mix of fear and hope reflected in the parting of her lips and the lifting of her brows.

Yes, the girl was good. If this was a performance, it was unmatched by any she'd seen before. No matter. Clara hadn't gotten where she was by playing it safe. Still, she hesitated. Her next words would change everything. In one version, she would have the last word and send the girl packing. The Clara Borges legend would stay intact.

But she'd played that scene her whole life. What if there was another version, a more original one, where she had a granddaughter and a family?

The seconds dragged on, and the girl's face fell with her shoulders. Clara knew it was cruel, but old habits were hard to break.

"I'm going to need a fresh pot of tea," she said at last, "if we're going to finish this book."

"The book?"

"Yes," Clara said, a slow smile spreading across her face. "I think it's about time I write chapter fifteen, don't you?"

From the Mars Hotel
Released June 1974

"U.S. Blues"
"China Doll"
"Unbroken Chain"
"Loose Lucy"
"Scarlet Begonias"
"Pride of Cucamonga"
"Money Money"
"Ship of Fools"

"Unbroken Chain" and "Pride of Cucamonga" are by
Phil Lesh and Robert Petersen.
"Money Money" is by Bob Weir and John Perry Barlow.
All other songs are by Jerry Garcia and Robert Hunter.

PRIDE OF CUCAMONGA
G.M. Malliet

One Tuesday in May, I stood on the scarred linoleum of a second-floor room of the Greystone Hotel, looking at the lifeless body of Mayor Ron Brayer. His corpse was six feet tall and hefty from too many fundraising dinners.

Having lived in Beachwood all my fifty-five years, I knew Ron Brayer—or thought I did. Most politicians are sidewinders; it's in their cold blood. But even though it's a low bar, I'd have said Ron was better than most.

I knew he was originally from Cucamonga, a fact that probably stuck in my mind because I used to drink its red wine, particularly the Sangiovese. Maybe I drank a bit more of it at one time than was good for me. My ex seemed to think so.

I knew he'd run on a liberal-leaning platform, and his election photos pictured him as a family man with two kids and a dog. I knew he'd married into one of the more distinguished families in town, because I'd gone to school with his wife. As Moira always seemed to be running for something, their pairing made perfect sense—in a Lady Macbeth sort of way.

Seeing as how he was dead, I tried not to judge Ron too harshly, but the scene in that room along that empty highway more than hinted at scandal. Disheveled sheets, for starters. A half-empty bottle of wine, two disposable bathroom cups used as wineglasses, a baggie half full of weed, an empty hypodermic.

He'd tried to run from his killer toward the bathroom—the

shotgun blast to his back spoke to that—and a big diesel truck roaring by at the right moment would have masked the sound of the shot. The hotel's owner—and understand, "hotel" was aspirational for what was essentially a roadside no-tell motel with a portico—was a Deadhead with long gray hair and a tie-dyed T-shirt in a rainbow of colors. Terry—we knew him down at the station as Terrence Albert Grey; just a bit of possession these days, nothing major—had called it in after a maid discovered the body. Surprisingly, he'd left the weed on the bedside table for us to find.

And then there were the photographs on the victim's cell phone, which had fallen or been kicked just out of Ron's reach. I unlocked it using his thumbprint, of course taking care not to leave prints of my own.

On it, I found intimate pictures of Ron with a woman who was not his wife, unless Moira had discovered the elusive Fountain of Youth. The woman in the photos looked young enough to be carded at the liquor store.

I had never put Ron on a pedestal. I knew the words "political" and "scandal" often went together. But this—the weed and the hypodermic? This smelled of a setup. As the sheriff in these-here parts, I reckoned I should go and talk to the man's enemies.

The evidence team arrived, and I left to give them space to work in that cold, narrow room.

Terry Grey was happy to tell me what he knew—anything to get the official cars cleared out of his parking lot.

"You guys being here is bad for business," he said.

I did not ask him which business—hotel or drug. "The man in 2B," I said. "Is he a regular?"

He nodded. "He's been coming here about two years. He signs in as John Smith and pays cash."

"Really."

"Cash is still legal tender in this country, last I heard."

"Especially when you pay taxes on every dime, as I'm sure *you* do. But he—let's call him John—was a regular? Every week?"

"Every Tuesday lunchtime, yep."

"And you never figured out he wasn't really John Smith?"

"I didn't care. He never caused any trouble. Even left a tip for the maid."

"You didn't recognize your own mayor?"

"Mayor?" Terry shook his head in what looked like genuine disbelief. "Now that's exactly why I don't vote. You can never tell with those guys."

I supposed it was possible Terry hadn't recognized Ron Brayer from his reelection posters. If he had, it would have been a situation ripe for blackmail. But blackmail took more brainpower than I'd credit Terry with having. He just wanted life to be hassle-free. His parents had left him the hotel, and so far he'd surprised us all by not running it into the ground.

"Was it the same woman every time?"

"Blond, fit, youngish. Yeah."

"Mrs. Smith, I presume?"

He shrugged. "I never met her, just saw her arrive a couple times. He'd show up first, alone."

"Every week."

"Just about. They broke up for a few months last year, then got back together. Or maybe they went away on vacation."

"Did you hear or see anything unusual today?"

He shook his head.

"Aren't you going to ask how he died, Terry?"

"Would it make a difference if I did? It's nothing to do with me. All I know is, I lost a good customer."

"For weed?"

Terry shook his head sadly: I had doubted him. "You know I gave all that up, Sheriff."

***

101

Back at the Major Crimes Division, I was saved from the tedium of tracking down the people who'd lost to Ron in the latest mayoral campaign by an anonymous tipster. The call led me to the Seaside Café and to Imogene Brayer, Ron's daughter.

She looked a few years younger than the girl in the photos on her father's phone, and my heart went out to her. She was still at the age when you believe everything your father tells you.

The age when you suspect he's a liar should come much later. And the age when he dies in a shotgun blast should never come at all.

I said the ritualistic words and meant them: "I'm sorry for your loss. This is a terrible thing."

She nodded, wiping away a tear with a paper napkin. I handed her a packet of tissues from my pocket.

"Are you sure you're up to talking to me?"

Another nod. "You have to punish whoever did this, and I think I know who it was."

"Have you talked it over with your mother?"

She gave me one of those looks they license to kids the moment they turn thirteen.

"I don't think Mom much cares who killed him. So, like, *no*—I haven't 'talked it over' with her. She's mostly worried about what her book club will think."

Under the circumstances, that was a valid concern, but perhaps Moira and Ron hadn't been getting along as well as his smiley reelection posters suggested. Did she know about her husband's secret life? Though the crime scene looked like a setup, it was clear he'd gone willingly to the Greystone Hotel.

"You know who Ivar Larson is, right?" she asked.

"Contractor? Builder?"

"That's him. You can thank him for those eyesore condos they built near Sealey Beach."

"I thank him every day when I drive past them. What's Larson got to do with your father?"

"Influence peddling? I think that's what they call it."

"You think your father was taking bribes?"

"I overheard a phone call or two."

"So—what are you saying? Larson had concluded his business with your father, and this was how he ended things?"

She shook her head. "So long as there's one square inch of undeveloped land in this town, Larson would want to continue the relationship. I think my dad wanted out."

And leaving drug paraphernalia behind after killing him would have been a good way to point the blame at someone else. It made sense.

Or maybe her father was being blackmailed all along by Larson, who used incriminating photos to sway Brayer's legislative decisions.

I had taken pictures of the crime scene while waiting for the team, including some shots of the compromising photos on Ron's phone. Before meeting Imogene, I'd cropped a selection into tactful head shots.

"Do you know this girl?" They were close enough in age that it didn't seem like a long shot.

"That's Rebecka. I see her around school, but I don't really *know* her. She's a year ahead of me and only hangs with the theater kids—the artsy ones." She framed the word "artsy" in air quotes and a look that told me Rebecka was not Imogene Brayer's favorite actress.

"I'll need to talk to your mother. Is she at home now?"

"I think so, yes."

"I'd offer you a ride, but maybe you don't want to be seen in a sheriff's car?"

"What, in case somebody thinks I'm being taken in for questioning?"

"Something like that. It's a small town."

"It sure is. Let them talk. Turn on the siren, for all I care."

When we left the café, the smells of coffee and apple pie were replaced by the ocean scent of brine and an inescapable hint of decay. I sent Imogene ahead to wait by my car and phoned my sergeant.

"Meet me at the Brayer house in fifteen," I told Harriman. "Anything from Margot?"

"She says he didn't die instantly, but he wouldn't have been able to call for help. It's too early for toxicology results."

"Traces of anything in the hypodermic?"

"Nah, it was clean. She thinks maybe never used."

"Fingerprints?"

Silence.

"You're shaking your head, aren't you?"

"Sorry, bad habit. I hate phones. Yeah, nothing back yet, but killers these days know to wear gloves. The *Daily Wave* wants to talk to you."

"Tell them they'll have to wait their turn."

I followed Imogene's directions past the eyesore condos to Marbella Lane, winding up past progressively grander properties to the very top of the wooded hill overlooking the town and the sea. If his daughter was right and Ron had been taking bribes, it was no wonder he needed the money.

Moira Brayer didn't recognize me at first. I wouldn't have known *her* if I hadn't known who she was: she'd had extensive work done to her face, which I'd last seen in person when we were teenagers. Now it had those prominent cheekbones made from fat injections, and her skin was stretched tight to her neck. She wore her long hair in a style better suited to a woman half her age.

I shared Imogene's opinion that she was holding up a little too well to be a believable grieving widow, but I uttered the standard condolences, adding that I would need to ask some questions.

"I thought so," she said, waving me and Harriman to a couch. "I have my book club arriving any minute."

My surprise must have shown, for she added: "Life must go on."

"I'll be upstairs," Imogene announced, flouncing out of the room and stomping up the stairs in a way that reminded me again how young she was. And how much at the mercy of fate, if her mother's attitude was anything to go by. I wondered if Imogene's inheritance would be used to pay for her mother's Botox injections, but from the look of the place, there was plenty of cash to go around.

Remembering Moira's family money, I wondered if it had been a bone of contention in the marriage. Public servants don't make that much. Maybe she got tired of paying the printer for the reelection posters.

"It's a funny thing," I said. "I know your husband was from Cucamonga, but I don't know much about his family or why he left there and ended up here."

"His father owned a winery. Drank most of the profits, if you could believe Ron—and I did, on that subject."

"So he came to Beachwood to seek his fortune?"

"He came here after college to work on a statewide political campaign. His candidate didn't win, but Ron liked the town and stuck around. He knew the political ropes, and when the mayor retired he decided to run to replace him. We met at a fundraiser, the first of hundreds, it feels like." She laughed briefly. "He told me he wanted to be the pride of Cucamonga—to make up for his dad's failure, I guess." She adjusted the diamond bracelet on her tanned wrist. "That particular kind of party never stops."

"It doesn't sound as if you were happy," I said.

"Are you married, detective?"

"I was."

"You're divorced?"

"Yes."

"I don't believe in divorce," she said. It struck me as such an oddly old-fashioned sentiment I nearly laughed aloud, but maybe she was trying to tell me something.

"Politicians survive divorce all the time," I said. "Why stay married if you weren't happy?"

She shifted uncomfortably in her chair. "My happiness is my business," she said. "Now what are you doing to find the person who killed my husband? They told me he was shot. I wouldn't have wished that for him. No matter what, I wouldn't wish that on anyone."

"It was a quick death. I hope it helps you to know that. Where were you earlier this afternoon, by the way?" Before she could protest, I said, "I have to ask."

"You look familiar," she said, avoiding the question.

"Beachwood High."

"Oh, my God, of course. You were on the football team."

I nodded. "Quarterback. Would you mind telling me where you were this—?"

"And you dated that redhead, what was her name?"

"Betty. I need to know where you were this afternoon, Mrs. Brayer."

"I was here. Ask any of the staff."

"You never left—not even for, say, half an hour?"

A maid interrupted us, asking where the book club would be meeting.

"Right here, Sandra. As usual. These men are leaving now."

Harrison looked ready to protest, but I cut him off. "Thank you for your time, Mrs. Brayer. Again, I'm sorry for your loss."

"What does she think this is?" fumed Harrison as we crossed the gravel driveway to our vehicles. "*Masterpiece Theatre*?"

"The rich are different from the rest of us, Harry. But we don't have enough to grill her right now. And according to the daughter—who I think would throw her mother under the bus if she could—it's a guy named Ivar Larson we should look to as a suspect."

"The Condo King."

"Imogene says he got where he is by greasing the right palms, including her father's. But the mayor didn't want to play anymore."

"Huh."

"What did you think of Her Ladyship? Is she good for this?"

Harrison took in the house, the grounds, the magnificence of it all. "I have trouble seeing her doing it herself. I don't know where she'd find the time between arranging charity balls and garden tours, unless she hired it out."

"Murder for hire? Yeah, I guess she wouldn't stick at that. The problem is, she's too well known around here to wander into a bar and hope the guy she asks to be a hitman isn't an undercover cop."

"I agree. Anyway, the thing is—"

We were interrupted by the arrival of another blonde with a resemblance to the one we'd just left, except this one looked like she spent a lot more time at the gym and less at the plastic surgeon's. An Uber deposited her at the door of the house, and I caught her before she could go inside, introducing myself and telling her I was investigating the death of the mayor.

"Isn't it awful?"

"Are you surprised Mrs. Brayer didn't cancel the book club?"

She laughed and waved a copy of *The Mars Room* in the air. "Not really. No one reads the book, you know, or even pretends to. Book club's just an excuse to get together and drink wine and talk girl talk. And today especially—who'd want to miss getting the inside scoop on a murder?"

Who, indeed?

"The group meets—what? Monthly?"

She nodded. "The husbands and boyfriends have learned to disappear on these occasions—oh, that was tactless of me. Poor Ron."

"You knew him?"

"Well, sure, he's the mayor. Has been for years—I mean, *was* for years."

She pushed back her long hair, and the diamond in her ring flashed in the sunlight.

"Are you and your husband both friends with the Brayers?"

"Sure, Ivar took a lot of meetings with the mayor and the council and the zoning guys. All part of doing business in this town."

"So you'd be Mrs. Larson?"

"Didn't I say? Yes, Kristi Larson." She held out her hand for a shake that told me her pull-up routine was working.

"We'll need to talk with him. What would be the best way to reach him?"

"His office is downtown. You want his cell number?"

"Please."

She rattled off the digits.

"Have you seen him today?"

"He's my husband," she said. "Of course I've seen him. But you're asking because of the murder. I get it. I don't know exactly where he was at lunchtime. You'll have to ask him."

Just then, a Lexus SUV turned into the drive, stopping to disgorge three women in big sunglasses and high heels. They were each clutching the same hardback as Kristi Larson, so I took them to be her fellow bibliophiles. I wondered what these pampered-looking women took away from a gritty book about female prisoners, then remembered Kristi's assurance that they hadn't read it.

"And where were you today, Mrs. Larson?"

The question took her by surprise, as it was meant to. I was trying to disturb her cool, detached mode. Most people involved with a murder, even at a remove, are excited by the prospect—if excited is the word. More like fascinated, and keen to worm details out of the investigators.

"I was at the high school. I coach softball and teach Phys Ed."

"And at lunchtime?"

She pulled down her sunglasses to glance at me. A flicker of annoyance made her blue eyes sparkle like her ring.

"I was probably in the break room, having my sandwich. Look, you're barking up the wrong tree. I rarely even said hello to Ron Brayer in passing at a party. It's his wife I'm friends with."

"Do you or your husband own guns?"

She didn't like this question, either. "So he *was* shot, then," she said. "My husband hunts. I don't."

"Thank you for your time, Mrs. Larson." I nodded at the book she was holding. "You really should read that. It's eye-opening."

I left Harrison with instructions to get contact details for the other women, who stood like a gaggle of perfumed geese on the steps to the house.

I took out my phone and searched for Kristi Larson, found her on Facebook. We weren't friends, so my access to her information was limited to photos, one of which was of her standing next to her husband and two children, all of probable Viking descent, on a ski vacation in what looked like Tahoe.

Her page linked to her husband's, and his banner and profile pictures made me think we could *never* have been friends. He was holding a twelve-gauge shotgun and hunkered down beside his trophy, a bull elephant.

Security at high schools these days is intense. You'd have an easier time getting an audience with the Pope. I flashed my badge at the woman guarding the principal's office and explained that my business was murder. She was suitably thrilled and eager to help and buzzed me straight in.

Iris Braverton's space was decorated with motivational posters bearing slogans like "Failure is Not an Option" and a beanbag chair for meetings with students. She was a woman in her thirties, painfully thin, with corkscrew hair and a band T-shirt that gave me to understand she wanted to be pals with her students. Patrol cops with that mindset last about a week on the job.

"You'll be wanting to know more about Mrs. Larson, then," she said. The hint of a smirk suggested she did not like Kristi Larson, and a visit from the police was no less than she might have expected.

"Not really," I said. "I was hoping to see her daughter."

"Her daughter? No, I can't allow that without a parent present."

"How old is she?"

"Rebecka is a senior, so seventeen or eighteen." She checked her computer. "Eighteen."

"Then she doesn't need a parent present for this. Besides, I don't want to talk to her. I just want to *see* her."

She didn't appear to have a rulebook that covered this situation, and after some hemming and hawing decided that, as long as I stayed right beside her, she would walk me over to the Potts Auditorium, where drama class was in session, and show me the girl. First, though, she put in a call to Ivar Larson and gave him the news.

"He wants to talk to you," she told me, handing me the phone.

"You're not to speak to Rebecka until her mother and I get there," said Ivar.

"Sure," I said. He wasn't prepared for me to be agreeable and spluttered a few unnecessary warnings about harassment. I pretended the connection was bad and hung up on him.

According to a bronze plaque beside the door, Lillian Potts—a grateful alumna of the class of 1983—had donated the auditorium to the school.

We found what looked like a dress rehearsal in progress, and I wondered why every high school in America feels compelled to produce *Our Town*. The principal pointed out Rebecka, who was playing Emily, the female lead.

She was the same girl featured in the compromising photos on the phone of the now-deceased mayor of Beachwood. From her composed demeanor, either she didn't know he was dead, or she was a believer that the show must go on.

True to my word, I was only there to look at her. Even in her long, old-fashioned dress, she resembled her mother, down to the long blond hair, the way she held her head, the athletic walk. Deadhead Terry wouldn't have been able to tell the difference, especially if he was stoned.

We'd have to get Terry in to identify the two of them, but I had enough to piece together what must have happened. The blonde Mayor Brayer had been meeting at the hotel for more than a year was Kristi Larson. Then they'd broken up for whatever reason, and the blonde he'd seen in recent months was Kristi's daughter, Rebecka.

It didn't take much to guess at a motive for the killing: Kristi was a woman not only scorned but trying to protect her daughter from an unscrupulous man old enough to be her father.

When we brought her in for questioning, Kristi agreed to be tested for gunshot residue. Her hands were clean, of course— gloves—but the clothing she was wearing had traces of both residue and blood spatter. She broke down quickly, ignoring my warnings even as her husband was busy getting their lawyer on the phone.

"You staged the scene, right?"

"With some drug stuff I'd confiscated from a student's locker, yes. To make Ron look like the degenerate he was."

"And the gun?"

"It's my husband's. I carried it to the hotel room in an equipment bag I borrowed from the softball team."

"You're not lying to protect your husband, are you?"

She shook her head. "He had no idea what was going on. I killed Ron so he'd never find out. About me, and especially about Rebecka. Ivar would have killed him." She laughed. "I guess I saved him the trouble."

"Kind of like in the book," I said.

"The book?"

"This month's book for your club, *The Mars Room*. Among other things, it's about the lengths a mother will go to protect her child. It's also about women in prison, which is where you're headed. You'll not only have time to read the book, Mrs. Larson— you're going to live it."

Blues for Allah
Released September 1975

"Help on the Way"
"Slipknot!"
"Franklin's Tower"
"King Solomon's Marbles"
"Stronger Than Dirt or Milkin' the Turkey"
"The Music Never Stopped"
"Crazy Fingers"
"Sage & Spirit"
"Blues for Allah"
"Sand Castles & Glass Camels"
"Unusual Occurrence in the Desert"

"Slipknot!" is by Jerry Garcia, Keith Godchaux,
Bill Kreutzmann, Phil Lesh, and Bob Weir.
"Franklin's Tower" is by Garcia, Kreutzmann, and Robert Hunter.
"King Solomon's Marbles" is by Lesh.
"Stronger Than Dirt or Milkin' the Turkey" is by
Mickey Hart, Kreutzmann, and Lesh.
"The Music Never Stopped" is by John Perry Barlow and Weir.
"Sage & Spirit" is by Weir.
"Sand Castles & Glass Camels" is by Garcia, Donna Godchaux,
Keith Godchaux, Hart, Kreutzmann, Lesh, and Weir.
All other songs are by Garcia and Hunter.

THE MUSIC NEVER STOPPED
Joseph S. Walker

Franklin's mind circled consciousness cautiously, testing for traps, ready to flee back to oblivion. A chopper nosing along above the jungle canopy, hunting for a secure place to settle. There were scary things in the jungle. Caution advised.

There were scary things in Franklin, too. Dark things. Memories, fear, anger. He kept his back to them, focusing on what he could hear.

Music?

His eyes opened.

He was in a tent that wasn't much more than an orange tarp flung over a rope. Morning sun shining through the vivid orange stung his eyes. His forearm was all he had for a pillow on the hard ground. That was all right. He'd slept in worse places.

A man and woman were lying on the other side of the tent. They faced him, both nude, the man behind the woman, his arms around her. Franklin had no idea who they were, and no memory of ever seeing them before. They were filthy, long hair matted with dirt and blades of grass, and he could smell them, the old sweat, the sex, the pungent warmth of their bodies. That was all right, too. He'd smelled worse things.

The woman's eyes were closed, but the man was looking at him.

"Did you hear something?" Franklin said, his voice a morning croak.

The man's hands moved across the woman's body. "I heard a

rainbow," he said. "How come nobody ever told me how much sound rainbows make?"

No help there.

Franklin rolled onto his back, thankful to find himself still in a pair of jeans, a t-shirt, shoes. He held his breath, listening.

He couldn't hear music, not with his ears, but somehow it was there anyway, moving through him from the feet upward, a lilting, bluesy, meandering song that didn't know how to stop.

Last night's music.

The festival had been announced a week previously, on flyers plastered over every flat surface in town. Five bands on a ramshackle, patched-together tour, playing in parks and fields and farms. Here, they'd be at Detwiler Park, a long grassy strip between the highway and the river, just outside the city limits.

Yesterday, the day of the show, Franklin and Avery stood on a street corner and watched the procession crawl through the city. First came five refurbished school buses, painted in bright blocks of primary colors and tie-dyed starbursts. Men and women hung out the windows, singing and waving, throwing strings of plastic beads and more flyers. A man sat on the hood of the fifth bus, stripped to the waist, his face crudely caked in white greasepaint, a smear of red across his mouth. He cackled, firing bottle rockets into the air. Sitting on the roof, another man sawed energetically at a fiddle, but in the din of the street his tune reached Franklin at about the volume of the wind through tall grass.

Behind the buses came two eighteen-wheelers, their trailers covered in spray-painted peace signs and musical notes, and then a seemingly endless stream of Volkswagen vans and rusted-out convertibles, mostly driven by unshaven men smoking hand-rolled joints.

Avery spit on the pavement. "Somebody needs to tell these fucking hippies it's 1975," he said. Across the street, someone with similar feelings in a second-floor apartment had put huge speakers in the window, and Led Zeppelin's "Kashmir" thundered down over the rolling nostalgia parade.

Franklin didn't say anything. Most times, it was better to just let Avery blow. When Franklin came back from 'Nam, Avery was what had been waiting for him. He was Franklin's cousin, the only real family he had, and he gave Franklin a place to sleep and things to do with his days. Mostly those things involved following Avery around, looking threatening. Avery was actually the bigger and stronger of the two, but he liked Franklin's aura. "You got that thousand-yard stare," he said. "Spooks people." Franklin was spooky enough that he never actually had to get physical with anyone, which suited him. He didn't want to open that door again and let the dark things loose.

Avery considered himself a gangster. He was the dealer people went to when all other options dried up, specializing in grass that was mostly seeds and stems, H that was mostly baking soda, speed with about the same jolt as a cup of coffee. Toss in some petty theft and the occasional mugging, and it was enough to avoid needing a job. He was, at any rate, too much of a professional to let his disdain for the festival blind him to a potential market, and the fact that his car had broken down was a minor obstacle. He elbowed Franklin and pointed at a powder-blue station wagon pulled into the gas station half a block down. "There's our ride," he said. "Let me do the talking."

As if there was any way to stop him.

A uniformed attendant was pumping gas into the station wagon under the watchful eye of the driver, who leaned against the pump, arms crossed over a small paunch. His dark hair was cut close to the skull, and he wore a baseball jersey and jeans that looked freshly ironed. He reminded Franklin of the guys who were always in the bars near military bases, guys who liked hanging around with soldiers and who were tolerated, barely, if they bought an occasional round.

"You going out to the festival?" Avery asked. "We could use a lift."

The man barely glanced at them. "You'll have to kick in for gas."

"Come on," Avery said. "Park's about ten miles from here. You're going there anyway, right?"

"Don't know what to tell you. Walking's free."

"Don't be an asshole, Trevor," said the taller of the two women coming from the liquor store next to the gas station, each carrying a case of beer. Unlike Trevor, they had dressed for the occasion, with peasant blouses over long flowing skirts. The one who had spoken wore sunglasses with tiny, perfectly round lenses. "Don't mind Trevor," she went on, addressing Avery. "He's in a mood because he's missing some game. I'm his wife Daisy, and this is my sister Liv."

"Avery. This is Franklin."

The attendant took the nozzle out. "Six and a quarter," he said to Trevor.

"You check the oil?" Trevor asked.

"No, sir. Didn't say you wanted it checked."

"Get the windshield, too."

The attendant looked at the line of waiting cars, sighed, and popped the hood.

Daisy put her case of beer in the back of the station wagon, tore open one end, and handed cans to Avery and Franklin. Franklin took a long, grateful drink. It had been miserably hot for weeks, and he was sure it was over ninety again.

"You guys are welcome to hop in," she said. "You from around here? We've been driving since before dawn."

The attendant closed the hood. "Six and a quarter," he said again. Trevor pushed himself from the pump. He slowly counted out six bills from his wallet, dug into his pocket for a quarter, and handed the money over.

"Tip the man," Liv said.

Trevor shook his head and got behind the wheel. "Gotta earn it," he said. He pointed a finger at Avery. "Don't spill beer in my car."

"You got it, Chief," Avery said. "No need to get nasty."

Franklin sat in the back, between Avery and Liv. Trevor shot away from the pump, nosing his way into the line of traffic and ignoring the honking behind him. At Daisy's sharp noise of disapproval, he snapped on the radio, cranking the volume when the Stones came on.

Liv nudged Franklin. He leaned over to catch her words. "You want to have a really good time tonight?"

Franklin didn't think that was possible, but he nodded.

"Close your eyes," she said. "Stick out your tongue."

He did, and something pressed against the tip of his tongue, a rough scrap of paper that immediately began to moisten and dissolve. He opened his eyes. She was holding a square of blotting paper with a corner torn away.

The radio snapped off. "Dammit, Liv," Trevor said, his eyes on the mirror. "That shit isn't free. Don't go handing it out to these bums."

"Bums?" Avery said.

Trevor didn't answer. He turned the radio back on and spun the volume knob higher. Daisy shook her head and looked out the window. Liv nudged Franklin again and pressed another scrap of paper into his hand. She pointed at her watch and mouthed the words "six hours," winking.

Franklin nodded. As soon as she turned to the window, he put the paper in his mouth. What the hell. Stuff probably wasn't any stronger than the shit Avery sold.

Franklin crawled out of the tent, his body responding to commands jerkily, reluctantly. He pissed against the tarp, watching the yellow liquid run down to be immediately swallowed by the dry earth. It had been weeks since they'd had any rain.

The whole length of the park was dotted with people. Some had lawn chairs, but most were on the ground in varying states of consciousness. Empty bottles and food wrappers and discarded garments were everywhere. An ambulance was up on the road, next to two police cruisers. Hundreds of cars were still parked in the field.

He turned in a slow circle. Down at the riverside, a few dozen people waded in the water, splashing each other. At one end of the park was a platform, under giant speakers hung from scaffolds. Men climbed over the makeshift stage, taking it apart and carrying pieces to the semis parked nearby.

Franklin still felt music vibrating through him. He shook his head and did the circle again, not seeing Avery or Trevor or anyone he recognized. He started slowly in the direction of the stage, afraid to simply stand there as his mind geared back up.

What had happened last night?

He sensed knowledge there, beneath the music, a darkness rising and threatening to break through.

At the park entrance, they paid five bucks a head for admission and were directed to the big field across the road from the stage. It was still several hours before showtime, but people drifted across the road with coolers and blankets to claim places.

They clustered around the back of the station wagon. Trevor took a beer from the open case. "This shit will be warm before we get through it," he said to Daisy. "Why the hell didn't you get ice?"

"They were out."

"Jesus. This podunk town." He didn't offer anybody else a beer.

"Thanks for the ride," Avery said. "We'll find our own way back."

"Damn right you will," Trevor said, not looking at him.

Avery tensed and rolled his shoulders. "You folks need anything for the show? Something to give you a little pep around midnight, maybe?"

"I fucking knew it," Trevor said. He looked at Daisy. "You got me giving rides to drug dealers now?"

"You already had shit in the car," Avery said. "Where do you think it came from?"

Trevor turned on him. "Get lost, asshole. Nobody here needs what you're selling."

Daisy put a hand on his arm. "Trevor. Be nice."

He shook her off and put a finger in Avery's face. "I see you again, I'll tell a cop about you."

Avery grinned. "Want to hear what's gonna happen if I see you again?"

Franklin got between them. "Come on, man. It's not worth it. There's money to be made here."

Avery moved slowly, keeping his head pivoted toward Trevor. "You telling me you don't want to hit this prick?"

Franklin wanted to hit people every day of his life. He wanted to hit Trevor so badly his hands were shaking. He wanted to hit Trevor almost as much as he wanted to hit Avery. He repeated the only thing he thought Avery would hear: "Let's go make some money."

"Fine. Whatever." Avery lifted his middle fingers in Trevor's direction and turned away.

For the next hour, Avery drifted around the park, chatting people up, offering his goods when it seemed safe to do so. There were only a handful of cops around, directing traffic and looking for obvious disturbances. He got a few takers, more as the show got closer.

Franklin didn't pay much attention to the exchanges. He mostly watched the men assembling the stage and rigging sound and lights. They were like a crew of ants, he thought. They all knew where to go and what to do, without being told. Franklin envied that. He never knew what to do.

That didn't worry him, though. And as afternoon crept toward early evening, it worried him less and less. When the acid kicked in, he discovered a fascinating new ability to walk on the air, his feet about six inches above the ground. He looked down, shifting his weight from one foot to the other, feeling the air yield a bit, like a mattress, the grass down there yellow and dry but ready to catch him if he fell.

He wouldn't fall; he was at home in the air. He wanted to tell Avery, but they had somehow gotten separated.

Impossibly far away, the first band started to play, and Franklin *could see their songs, ragged banners rippling away from the stage and dissipating in the crystal air.*

Some small part of his mind wondered if Liv's drugs weren't more potent than Avery's. That was the last coherent thought he had for a while.

Everything else before the orange tent was like shards of glass, each image sharp and distinct, but broken. Somebody gave him a bottle of wine. Later, he traded the empty bottle to a woman so she'd let her poodle tell him the secret of life. Straying to the riverside, he ran into three guys he'd gone through basic with who were later killed. They were watching the fish rising to the surface of the water to chase the swarming mosquitoes. He tried to tell them what the poodle had said, but they already knew and just wanted to listen to the show. He stood with them and watched the sun disappear in a pool of amber light and then the moon rise, clear and sparkling, into a sky of spinning stars.

When the last band came on, Franklin was right up by the stage, not knowing how he got there, holding hands with two people he'd never seen before, the music a net drawing all of them together. The singer stood at the front of the stage, just feet away, his beard and wild halo of hair lit with fire. His voice was Truth, and it pierced Franklin like an arrow. He felt the energy of the world running through him, beyond any description he would ever be able to provide. It seemed a music God Himself would exult in. Finally, it was so intense that he had to break away. He released the hands and let his feet come back to the ground and pushed through the dancing throng, away from the stage, away from the song that was lightning rolling along his spine, away from the music the band was channeling, not playing.

That's when he saw Avery and Trevor.

"Franklin," Avery said.

He was sitting on the ground, twenty feet in front of what was left of the stage, his forearms resting on his knees. His shirt was torn, and the hands hanging between his legs were red and raw. Franklin hadn't seen him there until he spoke.

"Where the hell you been?" Avery said. "I just woke up. I had a chick here, but I guess she ran off. Wild night, right?"

Franklin stared at him.

The dark thing in his mind was rising. He couldn't keep his back to it anymore.

They were at the edge of the crowd, walking toward the field of parked cars. Avery's arm was around Trevor's shoulder, and his other hand gripped Trevor's near arm. Trevor was staggering. It seemed almost as if Avery was dragging him.

Franklin followed, trying to decide how much of what he was seeing was real. He could see the two men clearly, but he could also hear what sounded like a rooster crowing in the middle of the night, and that didn't seem plausible.

Avery led Trevor back to where the station wagon was parked. By the time they got there, Franklin was close enough to hear Trevor mumble, "Jus' need to lie down. Need a rest."

"Sure, buddy," Avery said. He glanced over his shoulder and saw Franklin. "About damn time you showed up. Pretty boy had a few too many."

"A poodle told me the secret of life," Franklin said. He sat on the hood of a red sedan.

"Guess you've been having fun, too," Avery said. He propped Trevor up against the front fender of the station wagon, then went around and opened the rear gate. "Look at this," he said. "Got a few beers left. And, hey, a toolbox."

Trevor stood, nodding slowly, eyes lidded. Avery came back with three cans of beer held against his body by his left arm. His right hand held a hammer. Smiling, he smashed the driver's window with the hammer.

Trevor's head pivoted at the sound. "Hey."

Avery put the hammer on the roof of the car. He popped the tops of the three beer cans and, never looking away from Trevor's face, emptied them into the car, the warm beer foaming over the steering wheel and dashboard and seat. "Sorry, buddy," he said. "Looks like I spilled a little."

"Stop it." Trevor tried to stand upright. He reached for Avery and pushed feebly at his shoulder.

"You want to fight?" Avery asked. "Okay by me." He tossed the empty cans into the car, took the front of Trevor's shirt in his left hand, and drove his right fist into the middle of the man's face. Blood exploded from Trevor's nose, and his head snapped back. Avery held him up by his shirt and looked at Franklin. "You want in on this?"

Franklin didn't move or speak.

Avery shook his right fist and flexed the fingers. "Always forget how much that hurts," he said, and then he reclaimed the hammer and brought it down on the crown of Trevor's head. There was a cracking sound, and Trevor's body went limp. Avery let go of the shirt, and Trevor collapsed to the ground.

There wasn't much light this far from the stage, but Franklin could see Trevor's mangled face and the rivulet of blood running from his mouth onto the ground.

Nothing will ever grow there, *he thought.*

He could feel the dark things writhing inside him. He wanted to kick the body on the ground, feel its ribs cracking.

But he could also feel the music. He couldn't hear it. But he felt it.

He stood. Not looking at his cousin, not listening to his call, he ran back into the park.

Franklin turned away from Avery and walked toward the stage. He heard Avery scramble to his feet and call, "What's the matter, man? You still flying?"

Coiled cables rested in the grass to the side of the mostly disassembled stage. Franklin picked one up and got it on his shoulder and carried it to where men were lifting things into the two semis. Only one of the multicolored buses was left, parked between the big rigs. A burly Black man reached down from the trailer, and Franklin handed him the cable and turned to go back for another one.

Avery blocked his way. "What the hell are you doing? We've got to find a ride back into town. Had a big night, man. Got to restock."

Franklin shook his head and walked around him. Avery tried to grab his arm, but he pulled away and picked up an end of one of the big plywood flats that had formed the stage.

"That doesn't go yet," somebody said.

It was the lead singer from the final band. Franklin hadn't noticed him before. He was sitting on the back bumper of the bus, smoking a cigarette, wearing just sandals and a pair of jeans. His mane of hair was disheveled, and his eyes were bloodshot, but Franklin felt an echo of last night's charge just from looking at him.

"Boards go in last," the singer said. "Kind of hold everything else in place. You new?"

"Hoping to be," Franklin said. "I need a job."

"The hell you do," Avery said. "You work for me."

"We can probably use you," the singer said. "Seems like every stop we make, we lose a roadie or two. Can't blame them if they find somebody sweet, want to stick around a while. They can always catch up with us down the road." He gestured at Avery. "But your friend here seems to have other ideas."

"I don't care," Franklin said. He looked the singer in the eye, willing him to understand. "I still feel the music."

The singer raised his eyebrows. "That a fact?" He took a last drag and flicked his butt into the grass. "Well, then, I guess you better get on board. We're about to get truckin'. Got a long ride ahead. We can get to know each other, then tonight the boys can show you the ropes on setting up."

"Wait a minute," Avery said.

Franklin went to the open rear door of the bus.

"You can't do this," Avery said loudly.

Several of the men nearby, carrying things to the trucks, stopped what they were doing and looked at him. The singer scratched his chin. "Seems like he can," he said.

Avery said something else, but Franklin was on the bus now and didn't hear him.

Half of the bus had been converted to curtained-off bunks. Franklin slid into one of the remaining original seats. He heard the rear door close. The engine rumbled, and the bus started to move. Avery was outside the window, yelling something and slapping the side of the bus, but Franklin didn't see or hear him.

He didn't feel the dark things, either.

He couldn't lie to himself. He knew they might come back.

But right now, he just felt the music. It was endless, and Franklin knew he would feel it forever.

Terrapin Station
Released July 1977

"**Estimated Prophet**"
"Dancin' in the Streets"
"Passenger"
"Samson & Delilah"
"Sunrise"
"Terrapin Part 1" ("Lady With a Fan," "Terrapin Station,"
"Terrapin," "Terrapin Transit," "At a Siding,"
"Terrapin Flyer," "Refrain")

"Estimated Prophet" is by Bob Weir and John Perry Barlow.
"Dancin' in the Streets" is by William Stevenson,
Marvin Gaye, and I.J. Hunter.
"Passenger" is by Phil Lesh and Peter Monk.
"Samson & Delilah" is traditional, arranged by Weir.
"Sunrise" is by Donna Godchaux.
"Terrapin Transit" and "Terrapin Flyer" are by
Mickey Hart and Bill Kreutzmann.
"At a Siding" is by Hart and Robert Hunter.
"Refrain" is by Jerry Garcia.
All other songs are by Garcia and Robert Hunter.

ESTIMATED PROPHET
James L'Etoile

"You're nothing but a freak-show fortune teller." The fat man shoved away from the table, his hand clamped over an envelope stuffed with cash.

Malibu Jones ground his thumbs into his temples to quiet the uproar inside his head. "I'm sorry," he said. "I can't help what the voices tell me. You're going to die soon."

"You're an asshole," the fat man snarled, the buttons on his white dress shirt straining to contain his belly.

Sharp pain cut through Malibu's head. He shut his eyes against the shaft of light that illuminated the angry fat man. "You asked me to tell you what the future holds. I'm sorry. You don't have one."

The fat man shoved the envelope in his pocket and made for the tallow-yellow glass door. He paused there to look back at Malibu, seated at the table, eyes closed, both hands gripping the sides of his skull. "I can't believe people listen to your bullshit. I'm gonna tell the cops."

"No—no, you won't," Malibu said.

The fat man pushed through the storefront door, and seconds later car horns blared and there was the earsplitting sound of rubber on asphalt. A dull thud of metal on meat—and the pain in Malibu's head flicked off.

"Dammit, Mal," Rodney complained, coming through the threadbare curtain, "you're supposed to get the money before they leave."

"Rodney, it's getting worse. The voices are gnarly, man. I don't hear no good news no more. Only the dark stuff."

"Then effing *lie* to them. No one cares about your phony hoo-doo-voodoo shit. Just tell them what they want to hear. It's suckers like them pay the rent."

Malibu had the same washed-out feeling after every session. This one was worse and left the side of his face numb. He pulled himself from his chair, brushed past the six-three Rodney, and bent one of the blinds. Through the dusty window of the abandoned check-cashing store, he saw most of the fat man lying motionless beneath a city bus. A small knot of witnesses and the morbidly curious had gathered.

"I don't wanna do this no more," he said, his hands trembling.

"Get your shit together, Mal. You don't, and I'll lose everything."

"What do you mean, *you'll* lose everything?"

"I'm the one fronted the cash for this set-up."

"I'm the prophet. I'm the one people want to hear from. Not you."

Rodney grabbed Malibu by the collar and pulled him close, close enough for Malibu to smell the cheap body spray his partner used to cover his flop-sweat odor. "Listen, you little turd, I pulled you from that cardboard condo in Santa Monica. The cops wanted to 5150 your ass. You owe me."

"The cops don't understand my gift."

"Gift? You ain't got no gift. You can read people and tell them what they want to hear. This bullshit you're all of a sudden into, that don't fly. You feel me?" He shoved Malibu away.

"I can't help what the voices tell me."

"Don't play that with me. I don't wanna hear about no voices. I ain't one of your marks."

Malibu collapsed against the wall and slid to the floor, drained of energy. The pain in his head was gone, replaced by the listlessness that always followed his communication with the voices. It had to be angels' voices reverberating in his skull. If they were anything else—well, that was too terrifying to consider.

"We about to hit the big time," Rodney said. "You can't go soft on me now."

"No more," Malibu whimpered.

Rodney prodded him with his boot. "You ain't hearing me." He forced a sweat-stained news clipping into Malibu's hand. "We got us the score of a lifetime tonight—a whale."

Malibu unfolded the clipping, and a strange buzzing sensation vibrated through his fingertips, as if he'd grabbed a hornet's nest. Beneath the headline *Newspaper Heiress to Attend Charity Event* was a black-and-white photograph of a gorgeous woman in her early thirties.

"Her," Rodney said. "That woman right there is our golden ticket."

Malibu's fingers pulsed as he ran his thumb across the image. Her name, according to the caption, was Emily Jackson Carson. "We'll never get within fifty feet of her," he protested.

Rodney puffed up his bird-like chest. "You leave that to me. You see where this here charity event is going down?"

"The Beverly Hills Hotel. That's another reason we ain't getting to her. I got tossed from the sidewalk just walking by that place. They got security like rabid pit bulls, man. Count me out."

Rodney pinned him against the wall. "Listen here, you weak-kneed freak. You owe me. I made you what you are." He punctuated his diatribe with a finger jabbed repeatedly into Malibu's sternum. Each tap felt like a high-voltage cattle prod. "Man up, dude. Save the drama for this Carson chick. She's into all that, you know, crystals and chakras and shit. You can't screw the pooch on this one. If you do right, the word is gonna get around in her circle, and we'll be golden."

Suddenly Malibu heard the rustle of a whispered voice, so close he could feel its soft lips on his ear: *If you do this, blood will spill.*

He shuddered. The voice, though it carried an ominous warning, was soothing and loosened the tension in his head. She—it sounded like a woman—was trying to protect him.

Rodney sensed his partner's hesitation. "You want out? Fine. After this score, I'll get me another prophet. But tonight, you meet me outside the hotel at seven. Wear that suit I bought you—and take a shower. You smell like the toilet wine I made in Chino."

Rodney bulled his way out the front door, and Malibu staggered over and locked it behind him. A public works crew was hosing the last remnants of the fat man down the storm drain.

Malibu headed for the beach. When he got there, eyes closed and face tilted to the sun, he felt better than he had in days. The clean ocean air muted the voices and brought a sense of calm.

He took a deep breath and cast his gaze out on the blue horizon. The sun glinted on the sand and made the shore appear to burn in hues of gold and yellow.

This was where he needed to be, where Rodney had found him hustling tourists out of a few bucks telling fortunes. But now the camp he'd lived in had been torn down, his old tribe scattered to the winds. He had no place to call his own.

Rodney had promised to parlay his ability into big money, yet all he had to show for it so far was a secondhand suit his partner had gotten for him.

Malibu wanted out, but he needed to make a clean break from Rodney. Maybe he *should* show up at that hotel tonight. A nest egg would let him get away, find a place up the coast to squat. The ocean would keep him right.

One last score.

If you do this, blood will spill.

The voice sent a chill up his spine. He looked around wildly, but there was no one within earshot.

Get it together, Mal, he told himself.

Once last score, then find some surf shop where nobody knew him.

He watched the sun dip into the horizon, casting a fiery orange glow. This was his favorite time of day. He absorbed it, armoring himself against what lay ahead.

Back at the former check-cashing store Rodney had set him up in, he washed up the best he could. He didn't have time to sneak into the gym and steal a shower before they ran him off. A quick wipe-down would have to do.

He put on his once-white shirt and secondhand suit, pulled the cracked belt tight to keep the baggy pants from falling off his hips.

The newspaper clipping was where he'd left it on the floor. He picked it up, expecting to hear the voices.

Nothing, not even the vibration he'd felt before.

Scanning the article, he learned that Emily Jackson Carson had inherited her father's newspaper chain six months ago. The article didn't say how daddy died but hinted at friction regarding the future of the company. Investors worried she would carve it up and sell off the pieces.

The charity event was a fundraiser for an animal shelter. This high-brow socialite wanted to appear compassionate, and this was her way of showing it: toss a few dollars at a social cause so she could feel good about herself.

What had Rodney said? She was into crystals and chakras and shit.

Well, Rodney was right about one thing: Malibu knew how to read people. He knew what the Carson woman would ask him.

And he knew what the voices wanted him to tell her.

Two bus transfers and a three-block walk got him to the Beverly Hills Hotel two minutes late. Rodney was on the sidewalk, red-faced and agitated.

"Where the hell you been?"

"Calm down. I'm here, ain't I?"

Rodney grabbed him by the arm, pulled him close. "Dude, this woman is our big payday."

"How big? What's my cut?"

"Don't worry about that now. We gotta get in there before she changes her mind."

Rodney took a step toward the hotel entrance, but Malibu remained on the sidewalk.

"I ain't coming until you tell me how much I'm getting."

"Don't worry. The lady's loaded."

"How much?"

Rodney scowled. "Two grand."

"Two thousand dollars? What I gotta do for that kinda green?"

"What you always do."

"Okay, this one—and then I'm out."

"You can split if you want, but I'm telling you: once word gets around what we done for her—"

"What *I* done."

"Yeah, yeah, what *you* done. But don't forget, *I* put this deal together. Now come on, let's get to her bungalow. Number One, no less, where Marilyn Monroe used to stay. It goes for ten grand a night. We're in the big time now, Mal." He hesitated, put a hand on Malibu's elbow. "Hey, in case it comes up, I told her manager you work with the police as a psychic consultant."

"I don't do nothing like that."

"They don't know any different."

The hotel's interior gardens featured brick-lined walkways and manicured lawns. Lush bougainvillea gave each bungalow a secluded feel. With each step closer to the Carson woman's room, Malibu's head throbbed.

Rodney knocked on Bungalow Number One's golden door.

If you do this, blood will spill.

This time, Malibu didn't bother to look for the source of the icy whisper.

The door cracked open, and Emily Carson's light-green eyes peered through the crack.

"This him?"

"The Prophet himself," Rodney said.

She pulled the door open and motioned them inside. She wore a green silk robe, and her red hair hung over one shoulder. "Make yourself at home while I go change."

She padded off to the bedroom, and Rodney turned to Malibu.

"Look at this place, man." He stepped to a bar lined with crystal decanters and served himself a generous pour of bourbon. "Whoo-wee, this ain't your daddy's Jim Beam. Want a shot?"

"No, I'm good."

Emily Jackson Carson emerged from the bedroom in jeans and a Greenpeace T-shirt. She sat on a sofa and gestured Malibu to a club chair opposite her.

"Can I get you anything? How does this work?"

Before Malibu spoke, Rodney cleared his throat and propped himself against the bar. "I think we have some business to conduct before we start."

Emily frowned. "Tell you what: if I like what I hear, I'll pay. How's that sound?" Her eyes bored into Rodney's.

"How do I know—?" Rodney began.

Malibu cut him off. "That's fine by me, Miss Carson. But I can't guarantee you *will* like what I have to say. That's how it goes sometimes. The messages I give can be hard to hear."

She pondered that for a moment. "All right," she said at last. "I can live with that."

Malibu cringed as a shot of pain coursed through his body. "How can I help you?" he managed to ask.

She tucked her feet under her and said, "I'm being pulled in different directions. Can you offer anything to help me with the decisions I must make?"

The voices rumbled inside Malibu's head. "People will be hurt," he said.

"People are already hurting. I need to do what's right."

The pain sheared through his temples, and he clamped his hands on his head. "If you do this, blood will spill," he said, repeating the phrase that hammered in his skull.

Rodney grabbed his shoulder. "Get your shit together," he whispered fiercely. "Hand her some happy doodah ending, and we're done here."

The pain in Malibu's head sizzled, and he found it hard to breathe. "Sell it," he gasped. "Sell it all. It was your father's dream, not yours."

She nodded slowly. "Are you certain?"

"Yes. Then give the money away—all of it. You believe it's tainted by the things your father did to build his empire. Get rid of his blood money."

Rodney squeezed Malibu's shoulder angrily. "That's not what he meant. Tell her it's all good, Mal. Tell her."

"I know what the voices say. Blood will spill this day."

"He was a bastard," Emily Carson said softly. "He put so many small newspapers out of business. That might have happened eventually, anyway, what with everything going online, but he bankrupted people—ruined them. It *is* blood money, and I want nothing to do with it. Thank you."

She unfolded from the sofa and went to a desk, pulled a thick envelope from the drawer. "Here, you've earned this," she said, placing the envelope in Malibu's hand.

"I don't want it." He pushed it back into the woman's palm. "I didn't tell you anything you didn't already know."

"You helped me see things. I want you to have it."

Rodney grabbed the envelope. "You don't get to cut me out, Mal. I earned this."

There was a knife in Rodney's free hand, and Malibu grimaced as it prodded his gut.

He put his hand to the spot the knife blade had touched and

found that it had barely broken his skin.

"What are you *doing*?" the woman demanded, then hovered solicitously over Malibu. "Are you okay?"

"Don't worry about me. It ain't my time."

Rodney backed out of the room. "I think we're done here."

A voice vibrated in Malibu's head, and he repeated its warning. "You won't spend a dime of that money, Rodney."

"Save that shit for the suckers who are stupid enough to—"

Malibu felt a nerve impulse fire in the back of his head. "Rodney, don't do this."

"I'm locking down my future. No more small time for me."

Malibu shook his head. "You don't have a future, Rod. If you do this, blood will spill."

"Yeah, yeah," Rodney said. He shot out the bungalow door, bounced off a room-service cart, and lost his balance.

He fell over a wrought-iron railing and landed flat on his back. The railing sheared off and skewered him. Its broken end protruded from his chest, and blood spilled from the wound.

When Rodney breathed his last, the pain in Malibu's head instantly stopped, as if someone had flicked some cosmic light switch—and Malibu realized that his suffering hadn't been caused by the voices, after all. It had all come from Rodney.

He stooped and picked up the envelope and opened it. There was at least twenty thousand dollars there. Rodney had planned to short him once again, paying him off with a measly two grand.

He tried to return the money to Emily Carson, but she pushed the envelope back to him.

"I meant what I said. I don't want daddy's dirty money. You keep it."

Malibu heard one final voice inside his head: *You're gonna be okay.*

He wasn't sure if the angel meant her or him or both of them.

"I should get lost before the cops show up," he said.

"Do you have somewhere to go?"

Malibu took a last glance at Rodney. "I'm gonna head up the highway toward paradise," he said. "Wherever the ocean breezes blow, that's where I'll be. Don't worry, I'm gonna be okay. So are you."

And with that, Malibu set off. He was in no hurry. Oh, no, he had all the time in the world.

Shakedown Street
Released November 1978

"Good Lovin'"
"France"
"Shakedown Street"
"Serengetti"
"Fire on the Mountain"
"I Need a Miracle"
"From the Heart of Me"
"Stagger Lee"
"All New Minglewood Blues"
"If I Had the World to Give"

"Good Lovin'" is by Rudy Clark and Arthur Resnick.
"France" is by Mickey Hart, Robert Hunter, and Bob Weir.
"Serengetti" is by Hart and Bill Kreutzmann.
"Fire on the Mountain" is by Hart and Hunter.
"I Need a Miracle" is by John Perry Barlow and Weir.
"From the Heart of Me" is by Donna Godchaux.
"All New Minglewood Blues" is by Noah Lewis.
All other songs are by Jerry Garcia and Hunter.

SHAKEDOWN STREET
James D.F. Hannah

Because he's a philosopher, Ski says, "Used to be this town had a heart. Ain't got one now, though, no matter how you poke around."

But because he's also a rummy, positioned on the same stool every night at the Shaker Street Bar and Grill, no one pays him much mind.

No one except Beau, who stops wiping down the counter long enough to say, "What was that?"

Ski shakes his head and goes back to his Makers and Coke.

It's quiet tonight. Monday nights are. The drinkers are recovering from weekend sins, reciting empty promises like the Rosary, vowing they'll never do again what they did last weekend—at least until next weekend. They count on memories to be short, nature to be healing, livers to be regenerative.

Phil shows up at midnight. Phil, with his shaved head like a rifle cartridge, muscled arms a confusing tangle of tribal and Celtic tattoos, and that belt buckle, a silver plate the size of a hubcap, a skull and crossed swords on it.

He shoots a finger-gun at Beau. "How's it goin', Punchy?" he says.

Beau's already taking the envelope from the register. He'd like this to go quickly. "It's going," he says.

Phil thumbs through the envelope, purses his lips at the assortment of tens and twenties. He looks concerned, like a

141

high-school principal worried about your future.

"Feels light." He tucks the envelope into the back pocket of his designer jeans. "Been light the past few weeks, Punchy. I'd hate to have to tell Swerve you're holding out on paying your taxes."

Paying your taxes. It's a perfect phrase. Like the money's fixing roads or building parks—but really it goes to Swerve Mitchell, who runs the neighborhood, and it keeps Swerve from setting your building on fire or turning you into a suicide where the coroner's report claims you put the pistol in your mouth and pulled the trigger twice.

Beau produces a bottle of small-batch single-malt whiskey from under the bar. "See if this helps balm any aggravation Swerve might have."

Phil assesses the whiskey. "Yeah, that'll do it."

Beau understands the bottle will never make it past Phil's hands. It's simply the price of doing business. He's learned that everything's commodified—including survival. In the long hours he has with only his thoughts, Beau imagines a price tag hanging off the Earth, like a globe in a store. Because the world, it will cost you.

Phil sets the bottle down. A shit-eating grin creeps onto his face. "You know why they call him Swerve, right?"

Beau sighs. This will not, in fact, go quickly.

"I suppose it's because he's liable to do anything," he says. "You think he's heading one way, and he swerves in another direction."

"That's the story the old ladies tell. The polite one. No, the truth is, he was a kid at St. Ignatius, changing after gym class, and someone caught a glimpse of his junk." Phil plants an elbow on the bar and holds up his right hand flat, then angles it at the knuckles. "Seems it takes a hard left—pun intended. They started calling him Swerve, and the name stuck."

Then Phil turns serious. Pious as Sunday morning. "But you still ain't wrong. He'll do crazy shit if he thinks you're not playing straight. Keep that in mind, Punchy." He picks up the whiskey and fires another round from his finger-gun. "Hasta lasagna, don't get any on ya."

He's barely out the door when Ski says, "Might have over-played your part there, Beau Diddley."

Beau laughs. "You think so?"

Ski empties his glass. "Sometimes it's too much, too fast," he says.

Leigh shows up the next night. She's becoming a regular, fresh off shifts at the hospital, still in scrubs. She's a fine-boned brunette with a tendency toward gin and tonics and peppering Beau with questions like it's a never-ending first date. *Summer or winter? The beach or the mountains? Hemingway or Faulkner?*

Nothing's happened between them, and Beau's fine with that. He's not someone with many friends, and Leigh is a reminder he can engage past asking the customers what they're drinking.

Off her second G&T, Leigh says, "You a fan of the classics, Beau?"

"What do you mean?"

"Stories. You prefer new ones or old?"

"How old are we talking? Black-and-white movies? Stick fig-ures on cave walls?"

She twists her glass on her bar napkin. "They say the oldest story in the world is boy meets girl. It's how the Bible begins."

"If I recall Sister Mary Evina right, that story doesn't have a happy ending for the couple involved."

"Doesn't it? They only went off and started civilization. Be-sides, the great love stories are always tragedies. Tristan and Isolde. Romeo and Juliet. Cathy and Heathcliff."

"Them two in *The Notebook*."

Leigh's face curdles into disappointment. "We were doing so well, Beau." She swallows the rest of her drink. "Did I tell you I have an ex?"

"You did not," Beau says. "Though in the words of the poet,

what's your man got to do with me?"

"Not much, except he's one of those men. He does what he wants, and he gets what he wants."

Beau leans in closer to her across the bar. "What do *you* want, Leigh?"

The question catches her off-guard, as if she's never been asked before. It makes her dark eyes sparkle.

She taps the rim of her glass. "Another," she says, reaching into her purse for a pack of Lucky Strikes and a lighter. She touches flame to the end of a cigarette as Beau sets her drink in front of her. She blows smoke in the direction of the "No Smoking" sign behind the bar.

"I heard you did time," she says.

"Word travels."

"It's gotta go somewhere. Is it true?"

Beau pulls a beer from the cooler, pops the cap, and takes a long drink. "I was indeed a guest of the Oklahoma Department of Corrections. Ten years."

"Shit-kicker country. What happened?"

"It was during my boxing days. I didn't know it at the time, but it was at the end of those days. I was there for a fight. Two, in fact. The match itself and one afterwards, outside the ring. The second one, the other guy didn't walk away."

Beau watches Leigh for a response. She knocks ash onto a napkin.

"How'd you come to own a bar?" she says. "I didn't think ex-cons could get a liquor license in this state."

"Got lucky," he says. "The previous owner decided he wanted to move south, spend his mornings dropping a fishing line off a pier, his evenings chasing after grandkids, so the opportunity was there. I knew people, made some arrangements."

"Sounds shady."

"Everything sounds shady at two in the morning."

"Why here, though? You're not a neighborhood guy."

"I used to be."

"What changed?"

"The neighborhood."

Out of prison, Beau had tried to make a go of it out west. He went to California and thought about taking up surfing, but he hated salt water up his nose. Then he heard how easy it was to get lost amongst the trees of the Pacific Northwest—except they fucked with his allergies. Finally, he remembered the nuns of his childhood and the story of the prodigal son and came back east.

He returned to the gentrification he'd been hearing about in the news. Bodegas and appliance-repair shops gone, wine bars and overpriced boutiques moved in. The bridge-and-tunnel crowd now assholes living on the twelfth floor of a condo built after they tore down Beeman's Drug Store, where Beau had read comics and bought his first pack of Trojans. He wondered how many boba-tea parlors and hot-yoga studios and six-dollar taco stands one neighborhood needed.

And yet the Shaker Street Bar and Grill remained. Back in the day, everyone called it "Shakedown Street," supposedly because of the Grateful Dead song on the jukebox.

Yeah, right.

Shakedown Street was where cops and politicians and businessmen with "the" as middle names made the sausage of city life. Envelopes passed in folded newspapers and deals cut over watered-down drinks. Where Beau and his cousin and other aspirational malcontents had waited in the wings, looking for their own slice of the pie.

When Beau returned to Shakedown Street, he found the lighting too bright, the crowd too attractive, the jukebox replaced with the anonymity of a satellite-radio playlist.

He toyed with the idea of returning the bar to the way he remembered it, but he knew you can't shove the genie back in the bottle. Accept change and keep one step ahead of the dinosaurs, he thought. Know when it's a meteor coming at you and not a shooting star.

Leigh finishes her drink and says, "I should get home." She comes off the stool, and some bastard moves the floor underneath her. She catches the edge of the bar, steadies her stance. She grabs for her purse, and it topples. A pistol spills out, spins on the bar like a top.

Ski moves with a slow whiskey shuffle toward the exit. He opens the door and stares out.

"Dark there where the sun normally is," he says. "Must be because it's midnight." And he leaves.

Beau's eyes move from the gun to Leigh. "You're not in any shape to drive," he says. "Let me close up, and I'll get you home."

Ten minutes later, Leigh staggers to her Corolla with Beau at her side. Once he's buckled her in, she closes her eyes and rests her head against the window. He combs through her purse, past the gun, finds her wallet and her driver's license. Traces his thumbnail underneath her address.

He drives with the windows open, feeling the breath of the city wash over him. In prison, the air had always seemed motionless, a weight pressing down from on high. He ran laps, pumped iron, read in the prison library, but nothing helped. Even when the wind cut through the yard, stirring dust into spirals, turning into one of those Midwest storms where the sky grows dark and threatens to slit open its own belly to empty itself onto the earth, Beau felt nothing. The very oxygen in his lungs turned to cement, and he struggled to convince himself to breathe.

He wedges the Toyota between minivans in front of a block of row houses crammed one against another and brings Leigh out of the car. Small as she is, she's still a difficult ship to navigate. She has about a hundred keys on her keyring, and he tries each one—and of course it's the ninety-seventh key that opens the front door.

The house is decorated like four aisles of a home decor store, with embroidered pillows on the couch, abstract art on the walls, bookshelves organized by color.

He lays her across her bed, and she sprawls like an uncoiled Slinky. She's already snoring when the doorbell starts and doesn't stop. Someone leaning on the button. Beau's coming through the house when the banging begins.

Beau peers through the peephole.

What he sees is Phil.

The peephole distorts the world, but it can't hide the malice slithering behind the man's eyes like a snake through leaves. Beau knows those eyes from his time inside. Prison eyes aren't a window to the soul; they're a brick wall blocking the view into an empty room.

Beau opens the door, and when Phil sees him, his face contorts with anger.

"Punchy," he says, pushing his way into the house, Beau noticing the outline of a gun underneath his jacket. "What the fuck are you doing here?"

Beau moves toward the hallway door, blocking passage.

"Leigh was at the bar," he says. "She'd had a bit, so I thought I'd better get her home safe."

Phil's eyes scan the place like he's taking inventory. "Awful nice of you, Punchy. But I'm here now. I'll make sure she's okay."

Beau squares his feet and widens his shoulders.

"She's good. I think you ought to let her sleep."

Phil smiles with the warmth of the back of the freezer. "And what if I don't give a fuck what you think?"

Beau's first boxing coach told him it was the sport closest to chess. *It's focus and strategy*, he said. *Concentrate on yourself and your opponent. Look for their strengths, their weaknesses. Watch their moves and respond accordingly.*

Beau twists his torso, pushes his weight forward. His hands curl into fists. It's been years since his last fight, and he still moves with a muscle memory that never goes away.

Phil snaps his hand toward his pistol.

This is happening, Beau thinks.

Then, through the riot of blood pulsing in his ears, he hears the click of a hammer pull.

Leigh is at the far end of the room, in the other doorway, her revolver in hand. The gun's mostly aimed at Phil. Unsteady hold, eyes half-lidded, she's leaning against the doorframe to keep herself on her feet. If she pulls the trigger, God knows where that bullet's going.

Phil brings an empty hand back into view.

"Honey, why don't you put the gun away?" he says.

"Leave, Phil. Now."

"Can we talk, honey? Just you and me? You know we got something special. But those podcasts you listen to, the bullshit you hear at work, they're fucking you up."

"I'm not telling you again, Phil."

Phil's gaze turns to Beau as he backs away to the door.

"I got bodies on me, Punchy. You think I got a problem adding one more?"

He slams the door when he leaves. Beau turns the lock and watches through a window as headlights come on and a sports car pulls away with a squeal of tires.

Beau, still at the window, his body on alert, says, "You okay?" He glances back to see Leigh on the floor, the gun in her lap.

"The day of our wedding," she says, "he told the priest he'd love, honor, and cherish me. Tell me how well you think that's going."

Beau waits for the other shoe to drop. A few days pass with no sign of Phil. Nothing of Leigh, either. He thinks about driving past her place, checking on her, but that could be throwing gasoline on a fire.

Not every fight is mine, Beau reminds himself.

Tonight's slow, so he brings out the chessboard. He's playing

Ski and getting his ass kicked. Ski takes his queen early, and now he's running Beau's king around like he's going to steal his lunch money.

The game's already lost, Beau thinks, *and it's only a matter of time. But then again, so is every other damn thing.*

Ski studies the board. Sets his hand on a rook.

"Sometimes you think you've seen everything," he says, and moves the piece, and sips his drink. "And then you realize there's nothing left for you to see. I believe that's checkmate."

After closing, walking to his pickup, Beau's still got the game on his mind. He lost control of the middlegame, and Ski forced him into *zugzwang*—where any move only makes things worse.

He remembers one time in Cleveland, a fight against a kid that should have been over in three rounds. Beau was older, granted, but he told himself he had the footwork to move in, swarm the kid with blows, wear him down. But the kid had reach and speed he didn't expect, and he kept pulling back and nailing Beau with longer punches. He dragged the fight out ten full rounds, and by the end Beau was running on fumes and the kid was practically smiling.

Beau lost that one, and it hurt enough that he never felt the urge to go back to Cleveland. He figured most people felt that way about Cleveland, but still.

He's pulling his keys from his pocket when he sees the reflection mirrored in the truck window. A masked face running up behind him.

He turns in time for the crowbar to catch him just below the ribs.

Beau takes blind swings at the masked figure, but nothing connects. The crowbar comes down on his left forearm, and he screams and goes to his knees. The masked man drops the crowbar to the pavement and pounds two blows against the side of Beau's head with his bare fists.

The volume of the world turns to zero.

Beau's eyes rack focus long enough to see a belt buckle—a skull and crossed swords—and then everything cuts to black.

When they say you never forget your first time, they don't mean concussions, Beau tells the ER doctor. Forgetting concussions is par for the course, he says.

The doctor doesn't think that's funny.

Besides the concussion, Beau's managed a broken right arm, a few cracked ribs, and enough bruising to turn him into a Rorschach test.

He's waiting for someone to wheel him outside and let him catch a ride-share home when he sees Leigh in scrubs. Her makeup can't cover the bruises fading around her eyes and along her cheeks. Shadows of fingers stretched around her neck.

"Your name showed up in the system," she says. "Was this—?"

Beau nods. "Yeah, it was Ski. I beat him at gin rummy. He's a terrible loser."

There's a burst of laughter from Leigh, but it's gone as fast as a summer storm, and just as quickly she seems on the verge of tears. She sets her hand on Beau's.

"What should we do?" she says.

Beau doesn't say anything. He's still thinking about the middlegame.

It's near closing when Phil walks into Shaker Street.

Beau, arm in a sling, turns in time to see him take a seat at the bar.

Leigh's playing cards with Ski. She checks over her shoulder, like she's changing lanes in traffic. Her eyes turn hard for a second, then she goes back to her cards.

Beau says, "What can I get you?"

"Vodka tonic," Phil says. He motions toward Leigh. "What's

she doing here?"

"Probably losing," Beau says, setting down Phil's drink. "Ski's a shark."

"I'm surprised, that's all."

"I run a bar; she pays in cash."

Phil folds his fingers around his glass and sips his drink.

"You've looked better, Punchy," he says. "Have an accident?"

"Slipped in the shower."

"Thought after prison, you'd have learned not to bend over for the soap." He crunches ice from his glass.

"That's terrible for your teeth," Beau says.

"So is putting your nose where it don't belong. Hope you've learned your lesson. Now shut up and give me the money."

Beau leans back. "You play chess, Phil?"

"Nah. Seems like a stupid game. Why?"

"Because there's a term. *Zwischenzug*. It's German, 'cause you know Germans, they got a name for everything. It's when your opponent thinks you'll make one move, and instead you do something unexpected." He pulls a beer from the cooler and takes a drink. "I guess you could call it a sudden swerve."

The buzzer at the entrance sounds, and through the door comes a guy roughly the size and shape of a Bradley tank. Someone who's never bought off the rack his whole life. Face carved out of granite, wearing sunglasses after midnight. A Louisville slugger in one hand.

It's not until the man mountain comes around the corner of the bar that you see the guy behind him. This one could be the first one's silhouette, a shadow cast by the noonday sun.

Swerve Mitchell looks like he should be selling Bibles door to door. Thinner than a coke rail. Chunky black-framed glasses, his red hair cut short and combed sharply into place. White shirt buttoned to the neck, cuffed at the wrists, tough to tell where the shirt ends and Swerve begins, what with his ultra-pasteurized skin tone.

The man mountain pulls a chair from a table, its feet scraping across the concrete floor, and flips it to face Phil.

Swerve sits. Takes the bat from the man mountain.

Leigh sets her cards on the bar and watches. Ski considers his hand and lays down the queen of hearts.

Phil starts to speak, and before his words can find air, Swerve holds up a hand. He has long, graceful fingers, like spider legs, that could wrap around a basketball with ease.

"Stop," Swerve says. "You talking will do nothing but embarrass the both of us."

Phil looks at Beau, aims an indignant finger at him.

Beau's wearing a smile you couldn't remove with a sander. "Here's a thing you should consider," he says. "You tell stories you know nothing about, and you never consider where they came from. You ever stop to ask who called him Swerve for the first time?"

Phil's not paying attention when the man-mountain takes hold of the finger pointed at Beau and bends it backward until there's a snap like the crack of a chicken bone.

Phil screams. Swerve connects the length of polished ash with the base of Phil's skull. Phil falls forward, his nose smashing into the concrete.

Leigh gasps and covers her mouth with her hand. "Is he dead?"

Phil coughs up blood that puddles around his head.

"Not yet," Swerve says. He offers the bat to Beau. "What say you, cousin?"

Beau comes around the bar and crouches close to Phil's face, careful not to step in the blood.

"You've been skimming off my taxes," Beau says. "I write down how much is in every envelope I give you."

"And I write down how much is in every envelope *you* give *me*," Swerve says. "Because that's how we were raised."

Phil angles his head ever so slightly. "You two are—"

"On my mother's side," Beau says. "You'd have known, if you ever asked a question. If you didn't assume you know everything." He stands. "The world's got no memory anymore."

"I do," Swerve says.

Beau had taken the rap for Swerve for the fight outside the ring in Oklahoma, and when it tipped over into a manslaughter beef and Beau ended up in prison, he'd never spoken Swerve's name. Which was why, when Beau got out, Swerve had set him up at Shaker Street. Beau's stipulation was that he'd pay his taxes like anyone else. No special treatment. He wanted the anonymity.

But he also knew to write everything down. He remembered playing chess with Swerve as kids, how important it was to stay a few moves ahead of your opponent.

The man mountain jerks Phil off the floor by his collar. Phil, bloodstained, sputtering and choking for air.

"Go put him in the trunk, Leo," Swerve says.

Phil's arms flail, reaching for Leo and failing. Leo rabbit-punches him in the kidneys, and Phil stops doing much of anything but retching air as he's carried outside.

Beau and Swerve stand a few feet apart, like fighters in the ring. Squint, and there's maybe a family resemblance.

"Tell your mother I send my love," Beau says.

"You should come by for dinner, tell her yourself."

"I should," Beau says.

They shake hands, and Swerve leaves.

Back behind the bar, Beau pours himself a shot of vodka and throws it back fast.

"What happens now?" Leigh says.

"To Phil? He'll be a memory," Beau says, "until no one remembers him anymore."

"And what about us?"

Beau pours another shot and pushes the glass toward her.

Go to Heaven
Released April 1980

"Alabama Getaway"
"Far From Me"
"Althea"
"Feel Like a Stranger"
"Lost Sailor"
"Saint of Circumstance"
"Antwerp's Placebo (The Plumber)"
"Easy to Love You"
"Don't Ease Me In"

"Alabama Getaway" and "Althea" are by
Jerry Garcia and Robert Hunter.
"Far From Me" is by Brent Mydland.
"Feel Like a Stranger," "Lost Stranger," and
"Saint of Circumstance"
are by Bob Weir and John Perry Barlow.
"Antwerp's Place (The Plumber)" is by
Mickey Hart and Bill Kreutzmann.
"Easy to Love You" is by Mydland and Barlow.
"Don't Ease Me In" is traditional, arranged by the Grateful Dead.

ALTHEA
Faye Snowden

Quint had never been good with money. That was just a plain fact. He was good at fatherhood, and he had marriage down. When he was ten years old, he swore a blood oath to his sweetheart that one day they would marry, and he kept that promise. They wed in an El Cerrito church after they both graduated Berkeley. His daughter Sadie thought he hung the moon and flung the stars into the sky. And his teenaged son didn't mind claiming as father a man who shaved his head to hide a bald spot. But money, yeah, he sucked at that, and the oft discussed shit was about to hit the proverbial fan.

For the past few weeks, he'd been a regular at a cocktail bar on Durant near the university. He liked the fancy bartender in his black vest and bow tie, enjoyed the way he kept calling him "sir." The bartender had introduced himself several times—Lester or Sylvester or some shit—but Quint couldn't remember. He just knew that the guy was easy to talk to and kept his opinions to himself.

"Another whiskey, sir?" Lester or Sylvester asked.

"Sure, why not fiddle while Rome burns? Just put it on my tab."

A woman's voice, lithe and silky, said, "I got it."

Quint turned to find himself confronted with deep brown eyes staring into his. It was as if she were studying him to discover the best first cut for a dissection. A crown of purple and yellow wildflowers sat atop her long black braids.

"No, thank you, beautiful lady," he lied. She wasn't even two-beer beautiful, and definitely not another pretty face. Her smile, all straight white teeth against smooth brown skin, made her look hungry. "I've decided I won't be a complete cliché today."

"What do you mean?" she said. She took the barstool next to him, smelling of late-afternoon sunshine that reminded him of blue sky and clothes drying on the line.

"A married man in a bar, defeated and defenseless, meets a woman in a bar and further fucks up his already shattered life? Nope, not today."

"Hey, now, cool down," she said. "You don't sound too fond of yourself."

"When I tell my wife what I have to tell her, she won't be too fond of me, either."

She laughed and slid his iPhone aside to make room for two twenty-dollar bills. He used two fingers to push them back to her.

"Look, I ain't messing with you," she said. "I don't want to sleep with you."

"Then why are you buying me a stupidly expensive drink?"

"You first. Why so sad?"

"I don't tell strangers my business."

"You and Sylvester seem to get along well."

He wondered about that. How did she know he talked to the bartender? He had never seen her in the bar before. Or maybe he hadn't noticed her because he was too busy drowning his troubles in whiskey.

"My name is Althea," she said. "Does that help?"

It didn't. He kept quiet, hoping she would go away.

"Just open up." She leaned closer. "Tell me if you're wrecked or reckless."

They looked at each other for a few moments. The whiskey slithered in his veins like molten fool's gold, urging him to tell her. He hadn't even told his wife, yet here he was, ready to confess to some woman in a bar.

He knew then that he wasn't wrecked or reckless. He was both.

He remembered summer visits to his grandmother in Louisiana. They walked a lot, took buses. Quint was always terrified of walking across the Texarkana bridge. The short railing and the racing cars below put a fear that mirrored pain into his belly. When his grandmother asked why he was so frightened, he told the truth: *I'm afraid I might jump.* Her answer didn't help: *Don't worry, son. If you do right by the Lord, the Devil won't be able to tempt you over.*

He introduced himself to Althea as Quintin, ending with "my people call me Quint." Ignoring the old saying that *not all skin folk are kinfolk*, he figured Althea was one of his people. She signaled the bartender over to refill his glass, a long pour of the Four Roses he favored.

"I teach at City College," he said. "English 101, though I manage to sneak in a little Shakespeare now and then. Give them something to think about. My wife works for a tech company. She calls it glorified babysitting, but it pays the bills I can't. I've spent our entire marriage trying to figure out how I can make enough so she doesn't have to work."

"She doesn't want to work?"

"She's never said that, but she's an artist, a good one, and she can't follow that dream while working. I need to pull my weight."

"And so?"

"And so I trusted the wrong person, and I got burned."

He told her all of it, and she sat and listened. When he finished, the bar seemed to go quiet.

After a while, she said, "I see. You invested your life savings in your friend's tech start-up, and when he came around asking for more money, you forged your wife's signature and cashed out your retirement. You kept handing over cash, expecting bigger and bigger returns that never came. And your wife doesn't know?"

"I've been working up the nerve to tell her. I'm going to do it tonight."

"What do you think she'll say?"

"She'll be angry, disappointed, maybe even walk out. But she'll come back. She always does."

"Then why don't you just tell her?"

He twirled the whiskey glass between his palms, not looking at Althea.

She chuckled. "Pride. That's what's keeping you from being truthful?"

"I'm lost and ashamed."

She shrugged. "Shame is bad, but it can't get you drawn and quartered. If I were you, I'd be terrified of the one thing your wife deserves."

"What's that?"

"Justice. You betrayed her, and she's going to let you walk back into her life? Doesn't seem fair."

That was enough. Quint stood up to go, but the strange woman placed a hand on his arm.

"I'm sorry," she said. "I can't help thinking about your poor wife. Please, sit down."

He studied her for a moment. She did look sorry, and he wasn't in any hurry to go home. When he was back on the barstool, she gathered up her long braids and let them fall over one shoulder and said, quite conversationally, "If you take away the drama, the only thing you really need is money."

"As my southern grandmother would say, ain't you been listening?"

She smiled with every one of her straight white teeth. "Oh, I always listen. Listening is my life's blood."

"Okay, fine, I need money."

"Well," she said, tracing the rim of her glass with a red fingernail shaped like a coffin. "Believe it or not, I didn't come over here for a sad story."

He laughed. "Don't you collect sad stories, little Ophelia?"

She smiled and touched the flower wreath atop her braids. "I was hoping you'd notice."

"How could I not? Are you going to look for a puddle to drown yourself in later?"

He felt childish, but the comment she'd made about his wife still stung.

"What if I tell you I can not only offer you a little sympathy, but fix all your troubles?" she said, ignoring his meanness.

"I'd call you a liar."

"How much do you need?" she asked.

"A lot."

"How much is a lot?"

"Okay, I'll play. It's make-believe anyway, right, Ophelia?"

"Althea."

He started to calculate the amount in his head. He had already told Althea most of it—their life savings and retirement gone. What he hadn't told her was that, when his friend came around asking for even more money, he'd paid off a notary, forged his wife's signature again, and mortgaged the house.

"I need at least two hundred and fifty thousand dollars," he said at last.

"What if I told you I have a way of getting that money?"

"I'd say you were crazy."

"I have nine hundred and seventy-five thousand dollars waiting for me. I just need help getting it."

"Get serious."

"I am serious," she said. "That money is waiting for me in a house up the coast. It's from a divorce settlement."

"No offense, Ophelia. But you're not hot enough for me to get killed doing something stupid."

Something hard rolled into her eyes then, a gleam that wasn't friendly, one that said offense, indeed, had been taken.

"I know what you're thinking, Quint. You're thinking your life is over. But it doesn't have to be that way. All you need is money, and I have a way to get it for you. It'll be easy, a cakewalk."

"Then do it yourself."

"You don't understand. My ex is not being cooperative. I need someone to go with me. It's in cash, Quint."

He raised an eyebrow. "You got cash in a divorce?"

She grinned. "The IRS isn't very happy with me. If my ex moves the money into my bank account, those greedy fuckers would be on it like white on rice."

"Sounds reasonable."

"Believable," she said. "You mean it sounds believable. You're trying to convince yourself that I'm telling the truth. But you don't need to do that, because I am."

"Still not getting why you need *me*."

"Think of it as a friend asking you to go to her ex's house to pick up her things. I'm sure you've done that before. But this isn't clothes or a TV, it's money."

"And you'll pay me?"

"I'll give you two hundred thousand. Consider it a tip."

"You mean a tip if I help you rob him."

"It's my money," she said. "Mine. And he's getting off easy. I should get half of what he's got."

"You don't have anyone else that'll go with you?"

"Don't you think I tried? Everybody I know thinks what you think. They think I want to rob him. Or that I'm lying. But I'm not. I just want what he owes me."

"Call the police. Better yet, your lawyer."

"The police would make everything worse, and my lawyer is my husband's lawyer. I need a man to go with me. Someone my ex can't say no to."

She stopped talking. He sensed her waiting. He knew that the answer he gave would be the answer she would take. But he was a desperate man who couldn't say no.

That wasn't true. He *could* say no, but why should he? If he told his wife what he'd done, there would never be another moment when he could feel in control, never another second of hope. He decided to jump.

***

She hustled him out of the bar, barely giving him time to finish the last swallow of his drink. She insisted on taking her car and led him by the elbow to a shiny blue Audi parked around the corner. He insisted on driving and guided the beast through the Berkeley streets toward the 580 and over the San Rafael Bridge, the water moving slow and easy beneath them in the late afternoon sun, Quint feeling strong and powerful behind the wheel. Cityscapes gave way to groves of redwoods, and the narrow road became winding and full of hairpin turns.

Several hundred miles into the trip, most of which she slept, Althea directed him to a roadside gas station with 1980s throwback pumps. The attached convenience store jutted from the surrounding asphalt at an angle that was probably modern at the time it was built but now just looked sad and old. A red neon sign declaring "Lew's Place" signaled that it was open for business.

The kid behind the counter greeted them with a deep scowl, his nose twitching as if he smelled something that had gone rotten. If it weren't for his full bladder and the Audi's near-empty gas tank, Quint would have left. He didn't need or want trouble.

But Althea looked the kid straight in the face and said, "Hello, Smiley. Key for the bathroom?"

There was no answer.

"You mute? MAGA got your tongue? I need the key to the bathroom, or do you want me to shit on the floor? It'll be you scooping up the mess and scrubbing out the stain."

"Toilet's stopped up," he said.

"Just give her the key, man," Quint said.

The kid pulled a key with a blue plastic tag from a pegboard on the wall. He laid it on the counter and stepped back, as if he'd rather cut off his hand than touch Althea. She laughed, took the key, and headed to the back of the store.

Quint roamed the aisles looking for snacks, the kid following two or three steps behind him.

"Your camera broken?" Quint asked, without turning to look at him.

"It is," the boy sneered. "Don't need it, anyway. Consider me the fucking security camera, and don't steal nothing."

"The camera's broken like you are?" Althea said, suddenly reappearing.

"Hey, now," Quint said. "Leave the kid alone."

"Leave the kid alone," she mocked. "That's how you ended up with me, Quint: too much heart and not enough brain. That kid took one look at you and put you in a fucking box because of the color of your skin. And you're letting him get away with it."

Quint felt his face flame. "You don't know me."

"Oh, but I do. I know all about you. You told me everything, remember?"

"You two get out," the kid said. "Buy your shit and get out of here."

Althea laughed again. "You hear that, Quint? He sells shit. What's your name, li'l shit seller?"

"You fasten your lips and get your black—"

At that moment, Quint stopped thinking. Crazier than any imaginary Ophelia, the woman he had just spent hundreds of miles with was pointing a revolver at the kid. Mouthing a *pow!* like fucking Harley Quinn in Batman, she pulled the trigger. The kid clutched his gut and dropped.

"What did you do?" Quint screamed.

"Oh, my God," Althea said. "I didn't mean to. I didn't know it was loaded."

"Bullshit," Quint shouted.

"I swear. I promise. I didn't."

"You're insane," Quint said.

He rushed toward the boy, who was writhing on the floor in pain and crying. Crying real tears and asking repeatedly if he was going to die.

"I was just playing. I didn't know it was loaded. I swear I didn't."

Quint took off his black T-shirt and balled it up to put pressure on the wound.

"Don't touch him!" Althea commanded. "DNA!"

"He saw our faces," Quint spat. "Do you think DNA is going to matter?"

He saw the reality of the situation dawn on her. Before he could stop her, she shot the kid twice in the face, and Quint would remember the silence that followed the shots for the rest of his life. Not the kid's head exploding, but the silence, and then the ringing in his ears. He stared at Althea, horrified.

"I'm sorry," she whispered. "I had to. The money."

"Money?" For a second, he had trouble connecting the word to anything meaningful.

"We're close," she said. "A few more miles up the coast. There's enough gas in the Audi to make it."

No, Quint thought. He was not that guy, and he wouldn't let his family think he was the kind of person who'd kill for money. *Things* could be replaced. A life couldn't. He reached into the back pocket of his jeans for his phone.

Then he remembered.

In his mind's eye, he saw the phone plain as day on the gleaming bar. He saw her hand push it away from him when she offered to pay for his drink, remembered her hustling him out of there as if the place was about to catch fire.

"Give me your phone."

"For what?" she said, bringing the gun up so it was level with his chest.

"What? You going to shoot *me* now?"

"No, no," she said. "Of course not. Here, take it." She handed him the gun.

"Now your phone," he said.

"Quint, you don't know what you're doing. You want your wife and kids to be homeless?"

"What the fuck you talking about? I never told you I have kids."

"Yes, you did," she said.

"Or that I mortgaged the house."

"You did, but you were drinking, remember?"

"I can handle my liquor."

She glanced at the body on the floor. "If you can handle your liquor, do you think you'd be standing here with me right now?"

He didn't know what to say to that.

"A few more miles," she said quickly. "You've come this far. You can make things right with your wife."

God, he couldn't help himself. He still had that sliver of hope. The kid was dead, but he, Quint, was still here. It wasn't too late to save himself and his family.

Outside, he pulled his T-shirt on and smoothed it over his belly. The gun he put in the trunk. They drove. Sure enough, after a few miles, she told him to turn off the main road onto a smaller one that wound up and up. Soon they approached a multi-level monstrosity with great walls of glass. She told him to turn right, away from the house and onto a short road that dead-ended at a cliff overlooking the ocean.

He cut the engine and got out of the car. A cold wind blew salt into his face. He heard Althea crunching over the gravel behind him, but he wasn't paying her much attention. Instead, he was drawn to a waist-high fence made of two-by-fours and chicken-wire at the cliff's edge. It seemed to whisper to him in his grandmother's voice, *Why don't you want to walk across the bridge, son?* He didn't realize how close he'd gotten until the fence buckled. He snatched himself back.

"Careful," Althea said. "Looks like that fence is how the owners get rid of trespassers."

He turned to her. She was grinning. No, not grinning. She was outright laughing at him.

He knew then. Hope died. Everything within him, even fear, died.

"You lied," he said.

"Of course I lied." She doubled over with laughter.

"Whose house is this?"

"Does it matter?"

That was no chance meeting back in Berkeley, he realized. She had known things about him, that he had kids, that he'd mortgaged the house so he could invest more in his friend's doomed business.

And that fucking wreath of flowers.

He barely noticed the cliff begin to give way beneath his left foot as he worked it out. *Because I'm afraid I'll jump,* a voice whispered from very far away, a child's voice. Wasn't that what he'd been doing his entire life? Looking for shortcuts, taking crazy chances, jumping—and fucking it all up in the end?

Althea approached him, staring into his eyes like she had at the bar, until they stood chest to chest. And then she took another step. He inched back, his foot giving way a little more.

"When I mentioned the flowers in your hair, you said you'd hoped I would notice. You knew I was into Shakespeare before you walked into the bar. That's why you wore the wreath. You've been stalking me?"

"Now you're making the right connections. But much too late, Quint."

"Why?"

"You know why," she said. "You had your chance to say no, and you didn't take it. Your wife deserves justice, remember?"

"And justice is getting me to kill myself? You're stone cold crazy. I'm not jumping."

Her eyes went soft then. She placed a warm hand on Quint's cheek. The smile on her lips appeared sad but resigned.

"Oh, Quint," she said. "You still think you're the hero of this story."

She pushed him, and he screamed all the way down.

Althea's plan had been to lure him somewhere and shoot him in the head, kill him swiftly and cleanly like the others. But he kept calling her out of her name. Ophelia, indeed. He had pissed her off, and he deserved to be played with.

She drove the Audi back to the house and parked it in its usual spot in the cavernous garage. She walked through her chef's kitchen—gotta love that Wolf stove—and upstairs to her bedroom, stripping along the way. She showered and fell into bed and stared at herself in the mirrored ceiling for a long time.

The next evening, in the bar on Durant with a half-empty glass of Dom Perignon in front of her, she was still thinking about Quint. He'd been right, of course. She *had* stalked him, had hacked his financials. She stalked them all before the final play. It gave her the edge she needed, a way to hook them. She offered them whatever they needed, which usually came down to money, love, sex, or some combination of the three. She did it to mete out justice to the women they'd betrayed, those self-centered bastards who thought the world and its women were made for them.

It was a calling, really. She was doing Mary's work. In her mind, the Holy Mother was the ultimate wronged woman. After all, she'd been denied agency over her own body.

Althea looked up to find Sylvester the bartender grinning at her.

"Need another one?" he asked.

She smiled a predator's smile and tipped her glass to him. She knew full well he wasn't talking about the champagne.

In the Dark
Released July 1987

"**Touch of Grey**"
"Hell in a Bucket"
"When Push Comes to Shove"
"West L.A. Freeway"
"Tons of Steel"
"Throwing Stones"
"Black Muddy River"

"Hell in a Bucket" is by John Perry Barlow, Bob Weir,
and Brent Mydland.
"Tons of Steel" is by Mydland.
"Throwing Stones" is by Barlow and Weir.
All other songs are by Jerry Garcia and Robert Hunter.

TOUCH OF GREY
Kathryn O'Sullivan and Paul Awad

Marty Roberts gazed at Rosie painting in the soft early light streaming through the dining-hall window. The sun was Rosie's halo. Her purple caftan sleeves, her wings. Cupid's arrow had struck his heart deep. Marty hadn't felt like this about a woman in decades. Not since...

Don't dredge that up, he admonished himself. *That was over fifty years ago. Ancient history.*

Rosie dipped her brush, signed the lower left corner of the canvas, and nodded, satisfied. The canvas was awash in colorful swirls of energy and motion. "What do you think?" she asked. "I call it *Morning Sky*."

"I don't know how you do it," he said with admiration. "All I can do is paint by numbers. You're amazing."

"Nonsense," Rosie said, with a dismissive wave.

But he could tell she was pleased as she grinned and squinted into the light.

"Want me to pull the curtains?" he asked.

"If you'd like. It's the cataracts that make the damn glare worse."

Marty rose, his knees aching.

The running club, glistening with sweat, trickled into the dining room and threw smug looks their way. Marty glanced at the wall clock and automatically subtracted five minutes. As long as he'd lived in the Sunrise Ponds Senior Village, the clocks in the

171

community center had run late. Maybe the staff thought it gave the residents the illusion of a few extra minutes of life.

"Time to pack up," he said. "The Ables have arrived." The Ables was the nickname they gave to residents who flaunted their ability to move without the aid of walker or cane.

Rosie rolled her eyes. "I don't see why I can't leave my stuff here."

Marty suppressed a grin. One thing Rosie hated was rules. And not painting in the dining room during meals was one of the rules.

"I was thinking of requesting a move to Room 17," Marty said, helping Rosie pack. The room's previous resident—ninety-year-old Mr. Fry—had recently moved to the assisted-living building, and his old room's unobstructed view of the gazebo and pond made it a prized location. It was also next to Rosie's apartment, which would put Marty a few steps closer to solidifying their budding romance.

"Didn't you hear?" Rosie said. "Room 17 has been taken. A new resident's moving in today."

Marty tried to hide his disappointment.

She leaned close enough for him to smell her patchouli and whispered, "And he's a celebrity."

Marty swallowed. "A celebrity?"

She zipped up her bag of brushes and paints. "Carl something. He was the singer in that band. What was their name? Sugar—"

Venom coursed through Marty's veins. "Sugar Spree?"

"Yes, that's it. They had that fab song, 'Traces of Silver.'" Rosie sang, "'Traces of silver on a cloudy day. Memories linger, fog on San Francisco Bay.'"

Marty's heart pounded in his ears and drowned out the singing. But it didn't matter. He knew the lyrics, had co-written them with Carl Unger before Sugar Spree's split. The song had been a Billboard Hot 100 hit, peaking at number nine and generating a worldwide following. By the time it dropped, though, Carl had kicked Marty out of the band. His reason, rumor had it, was that

Marty had pushed the group in a direction that alienated loyal fans. But Marty knew the truth. Carl wanted the money and Bonnie for himself. Marty's contribution to the lyrics hadn't been credited on the song, so he'd been denied the recognition and riches that had gone to Carl and Carl alone. Devastated by the betrayal, Marty had never written any further songs.

Carl had stolen his words and his girlfriend. And now he was stealing his room.

Marty stared at the number 17 on the door. Music blared from within. He swallowed, pushing down the bitterness that bubbled in his belly. He retrieved a tattered index card from his wallet, the fifteen grievances he had committed to paper over fifty years ago. The grievances he had long dreamed of reciting to Carl. Carl, the front man. Carl, the lady's man. Carl, Carl, Carl. Marty's throat filled with bile. He resisted the urge to spit.

Marty and Carl had met in the Army, when they were both just legal to vote and drink. They'd quickly discovered a mutual knack for music and a mutual ineptitude for military life. They lasted eighteen months in uniform and got out before the government started drafting kids for Vietnam. Marty was discharged for his bad back, Carl for his bad behavior.

After their discharge, they moved to San Francisco's Haight-Ashbury district and formed Sugar Spree. Carl was lead guitar and vocals, Marty bass. Then came their first record deal. They lived together with their bandmates and a revolving door of groupies. Good friends. Good music. Good times. For a while...

Marty scanned his list of grievances. Number One was Bonnie, a back-up singer and his first love. He'd adored her, told her she was his muse. Time had faded Bonnie's image in his mind like an old photo, but Carl's betrayal was crystal-clear. It was time to settle the score.

He squeezed the card in his right hand and raised his left. But before he could knock, the door flung open, and there was Carl in a billowing marijuana haze, all *Reefer Madness*.

"What can I do for you, brother?" Carl asked in a long exhalation of smoke. A guitar wailed from the stereo.

Marty froze, his mind struggling to adjust to the Carl before him. Even though it had been decades since their last encounter, Marty had ludicrously expected to see the handsome and lean front man of Sugar Spree. That was the man frozen in the amber recesses of his memory. But Carl's gorgeous head of brown hair was now just a fringe of snow white pulled into a wispy ponytail around a liver-spotted skull, his face deeply lined, his belly straining the buttons of his Hawaiian shirt.

Carl studied Marty, no sign of recognition in his bloodshot eyes. He took another long drag. "Let me guess," he said. "You want me to turn down the music."

"For starters," Marty yelled.

Carl shook his head. "That didn't take long." He walked to the vintage turntable and dialed the volume to zero. "These retirement cribs are all the same. Everyone always complaining about the music, the smoke. That's what got me kicked out of the last three places." He plopped onto a well-worn sofa, threw his feet up on a stack of unpacked boxes, and gazed at Marty. "Go ahead, brother. Lay it on me."

Marty stared down at Carl, stunned. Carl apparently thought Marty was just an irksome neighbor, didn't recognize his onetime friend and collaborator. He looked at the index card in his fist. *Get it together, Marty. Focus.* He cleared his throat to speak.

Carl frowned. "Hey, do I know you from somewhere?"

Years of suppressed rage boiled to the surface, and Marty took a breath to steady himself. "It's me," he said. "Marty!"

Carl squinted. "Marty? Marty Roberts? Man, I thought you were dead."

Marty glared. "Well, I'm not."

Carl stubbed out his joint in an ashtray. "Didn't know you at first, brother. You got old."

"*I* got old?" Marty snapped.

"It's all right," Carl said, raising his hands in surrender. "It suits you." He grinned and tugged at his white ponytail. "I got a touch of gray myself." He motioned to a chair. "Take a load off. Tell me how you've been."

"I'm not here to catch up." Marty peered at his card. "I have a few things to say to you."

"What you got there?" Carl asked.

"A list of grievances."

"Don't tell me you're still upset about being kicked out of the band. Come on. We were kids, Marty." Carl looked at him with pity and sighed. "Clearly, this is something you feel you have to do." He motioned for Marty to continue. "Say your piece and then get out. You're harshing my mellow."

Marty cleared his throat, but a knock on the open door interrupted him.

Rosie stood in the entrance, a plate of brownies in hand. "You boys mind if I come in?" she asked.

Carl gave her the once-over. "Not at all. Have a seat. Are those for me?"

"I wanted to be the first to welcome you, but it looks like Marty beat me to it." She set the plate on the boxes. "I'm Rosie Temple. I baked brownies for you."

Carl took her hand and kissed it. "How thoughtful. They wouldn't happen to be *special* brownies, would they?"

Carl winked and, to Marty's horror, Rosie giggled like a smitten teen.

She slapped Carl's hand as if scolding him. "I can see you're a troublemaker."

"I hope that's not a problem for you, doll," Carl said with a smirk, then caught Marty glaring at him.

"I don't mind. We could use a little excitement around here. Couldn't we, Marty?"

Marty forced a smile, but jealous thoughts screamed like banshees inside his head.

"You two know each other, I see," Carl said.

"Marty and I are friends."

"Marty and I are friends, too," Carl said. "He was about to tell me something important."

Rosie gazed at Marty. "Really? What's that?"

Carl flashed a wicked grin. Marty's hands closed into fists.

"It can wait," Marty said, and he strode out of Room 17.

Rage coursed through Marty's body. His skin felt like fire. He replayed his encounter with Carl and winced. Every exchange felt like nails on chalkboard. He grabbed a Coors from the fridge and chugged until it was empty. He needed to chill. After all, he had to prepare jambalaya for his weekly dinner with Rosie.

Marty grabbed the celery. As he rinsed the stalks, he imagined Carl's neck in his hands and twisted until they cracked. Marty tossed the mutilated vegetable in the garbage, chopped two new stalks, and scraped them into the pot. An image of Carl sitting with Rosie on the sofa flashed through his mind. He snatched a lemon, pictured Carl's heart, and squeezed until his fingers pierced the rind and juice oozed out. *Get it together. Rosie's coming over. Do you want her to see you like this?* But it was no use. All he could think about was Carl. The sooner he was disposed of, the better.

He gazed out the kitchen window through the trees at the sun setting over the pond. Perhaps he could poison Carl's beloved weed with pesticide. But how would he get access to Carl's stash without being discovered? Or he could spike the bum's soda with high-dose caffeine pills and induce a heart attack. But what if Carl recovered? And, worse yet, had Rosie nurse him back to health?

He watched the sun disappear behind the pond's gazebo, and then it clicked. The gazebo. Of course. He'd make it look like Carl struck his head in a drunken stupor. A tragic accident. Hardly unexpected, given Carl's life in the fast lane.

Marty grinned. *Poor Carl. He won't know what hit him.*

***

Marty waited in the gazebo that projected over the water of the village's pond. A decorative terrapin statue perched on the built-in bench. Normally, the shelter was aglow with lights, like a scene in a Hallmark Christmas movie, but he'd unplugged the string of bulbs and unscrewed the security lights.

He hadn't slept well after last night's dinner with Rosie. Why hadn't Marty told her he'd been a member of Sugar Spree? What was Carl like back then? Was Carl always so funny? Did he have groupies? And on and on. Marty's vague answers had satisfied her. It was clear she was more interested in basking in her encounter with a celebrity than knowing what had really happened with the band. The conversation solidified the urgency of Carl's demise.

Now all Marty needed was for Carl to take the bait. Early this morning, he'd slipped a note under Room 17's door:

Carl, I'm trying to show a little grace, but I simply must meet you face to face. It would give me much elation if you would meet me in the gazebo for a midnight assignation.

Your fan, Rosie

Boards creaked on the pier. Marty ducked behind a column, squeezed the whiskey bottle in his hand, and watched Carl lope toward the gazebo, humming. If all went according to plan, tonight Carl would hum his last tune.

As Carl entered the gazebo, Marty stepped from the shadows. "I knew you'd show up," he said, clutching the bottle. "I knew you'd come here to meet Rosie."

"Have you seen her?" Carl asked. Then he noticed Marty's glare. "You got a problem with me making time with a new friend?"

The way Carl said *friend* made Marty sick. "I don't want you being *friends* with Rosie."

"Wait a second." Carl held up the note Marty had slipped under his door. "You wrote this, didn't you?"

Marty's jaw clenched.

Carl chuckled. "I should have known."

"What's that supposed to mean?" Marty said.

Carl removed a pair of glasses from his shirt pocket and shined his phone's flashlight at the note. He read, "'It would give me much elation, if you'd meet me in the gazebo for a midnight ass...ig...nation.'" He tapped off the light. "You always had that big vocabulary, Marty, even when we were kids. The only words I knew were obscene. 'Assignation'? I had to look that one up."

"So you came to hook up with Rosie," Marty said.

"Of course." Carl gestured to his crotch. "This dog hasn't been fed in years."

Marty curled his lip in disgust. "Is that what happened with Bonnie? Was she just a skirt to you?"

"Bonnie?" Carl said, surprised. "I haven't heard that name in years." He noticed the whiskey bottle in Marty's hand. "Say, brother, what you got there? A bit of the red eye? Is that what you want? Kick back a few and talk it out? Why didn't you say so? Well, let me have it." He motioned for Marty to hand him the liquor.

Marty raised the bottle and swung toward Carl's head. But Carl stepped to the side and swatted Marty's arm, sending the bottle rolling to the ground.

"You crazy?" Carl shouted.

Marty lunged for the stone terrapin, but Carl grabbed his shirt before he could reach it.

The two grunted as they tussled. Then Carl's knee buckled. He groaned and toppled against the bench. Marty felt his shoulder pop and let out a groan of his own. He crawled to Carl on his good arm and slapped Carl's face. Carl took off a shoe and pounded Marty's back. The two men scuffled until, exhausted, they flopped onto their backs, huffing and puffing. They gazed at one another, bloody and spent, and it was as if they were kids in boot camp again, before the band, when they had first discovered their shared love of music.

Carl forced himself to a sitting position and glanced at Marty. "Look at us." He laughed, then moaned and clutched his ribs.

Marty noticed Carl was missing a front canine tooth. "Sorry about that."

Carl ran his tongue around his mouth and spit the tooth out. "I'll get by."

Marty stared at his onetime friend with a sudden insight. All these years he had blamed Carl for the loss of Bonnie, his muse, and with her the loss of his ability to put together lyrics. But Bonnie had never been his muse. It had always been Carl. It was the pressure, the tension in their relationship, that had created the diamonds.

A lyric popped into Marty's head. He sat up. Then came another. Rhymes about friends and growing older and survival.

"You still got my note?" Marty said, his heart racing.

"Sure," Carl said. He handed Marty the paper.

Marty unfolded it and turned it over. He took a pen from his pocket and scribbled.

"I know that look," Carl said, excitement in his voice. "You got a song."

Marty nodded and kept writing.

"How about some whiskey for inspiration?" Carl said. "Where's that hooch?" He retrieved the unbroken bottle, twisted the cap off, and swigged. He handed it to Marty.

Marty took a sip. Carl removed a joint from his shirt pocket and winked. Marty laughed, took another sip, and resumed writing.

The words flowed with such ease that Marty found himself giggling. Carl hummed potential melodies. They sat that way, by the light of Marty's cellphone, laughing like children as the years of resentment and animosity faded away. By the time Marty reached the final chorus, everything was all right. They were all right. There was a silver lining to Carl's arrival at Sunrise Ponds, after all.

"So, let me see the masterpiece," Carl said.

Marty handed the paper to Carl. Carl read the scrawled words and whistled through his teeth. "You make it look easy as ABC," he said. "This is gold. We should get the band back together—what's left of us—and record a new album."

Marty smiled, pleased. For the first time in a long time, he felt relaxed and free.

Carl grunted as he shifted his weight. "We should go inside. Check out the damage. Here, I'll give you a hand."

Carl stood. Marty reached for his hand, but the next thing he knew, Carl was swinging the terrapin statue at his head. It hit his temple hard, and he toppled back against the railing.

"What the hell?" he said, stunned.

Carl grinned. "This trip down Memory Lane's been fun, Marty, but it's time to move on. Thanks for the song. I'm sure Rosie will love it."

Before Marty could respond, Carl charged and shoved him in the chest. Marty flipped over the railing and flailed helplessly in the water. The last thing he saw in the descending dark was Carl tucking the paper in his pocket.

As he went under, he realized Carl had done it again. He had stolen his song. And he would steal Rosie, too.

Built to Last
Released October 1989

"Foolish Heart"
"Just a Little Light"
"Built to Last"
"Blow Away"
"Victim or the Crime"
"We Can Run"
"Standing on the Moon"
"Picasso Moon"
"I Will Take You Home"

"Just a Little Light," "Blow Away," "We Can Run,"
and "I Will Take You Home"
are by John Perry Barlow and Brent Mydland.
"Victim or the Crime" is by Gerrit Graham and Bob Weir.
"Picasso Moon" is by Barlow, Bob Bralove, and Weir.
All other songs are by Jerry Garcia and Robert Hunter.

VICTIM OR THE CRIME
Bruce Robert Coffin

Rookie NYPD patrolman Jerry Weir was doing his best to stay focused. Graveyard shifts in the Big Apple weren't any different than anywhere else, he supposed: prowling around at all hours of the night in a blue-and-white, attempting to balance law and order. But when daybreak rolled around, things tended to get a bit dicey.

Weir happened upon the murder while making his morning rounds. As was his routine, he cruised Little Italy's business district prior to shift change. Failure to discover an overnight burglary at one of the downtown establishments in your assigned sector was considered bad form by the Powers That Be, and it was a far greater sin if someone else—like the owner of said establishment—discovered the break-in first. It was expected that obvious things like missing windows or forced doors would be noticed, whether or not the business was alarmed. Crimes missed were a black eye to the career aspirations of the officer responsible.

Weir, though still wet behind the ears, was a dedicated cop who aspired to rise in the department. Who knew what rank he might attain? Sergeant or even detective first class. Twenty-five years would be a long time to push a radio car.

Dawn had yet to break when Weir was flagged down at a red light by a harried middle-aged man in a blue tracksuit.

"What seems to be the problem, sir?"

"Murder," the man said, pointing in the direction of Rizzi's bodega.

Weir jerked his squad car to the curb near the front of the popular neighborhood market, ordered the witnesses to remain on the sidewalk, and hurried inside. Franklin Rizzoli, the owner, was lying behind the counter in a puddle of blood, face up on the painted concrete floor. The front of Rizzoli's white apron looked like it had been tie-dyed crimson, and the man's head hadn't fared much better. Weir grabbed the portable microphone clipped to his epaulet and called for backup.

"5 Charlie 7, I need backup assistance and a bus at Rizzi's, corner of Mulberry and Hester. At least one gunshot victim. Expedite."

"Ten-four, 5 Charlie 7."

The first rule of any crime scene is to make sure it's safe and there are no other victims. Weir slid his sidearm from its holster. He needed to be sure the killer wasn't hiding nearby. One of his training officers had been fond of saying, "Nothing ruins a perfectly good overnight shift quicker than getting shot."

He made a thorough sweep of the store and its walk-in coolers but turned up nothing. The last thing he checked was the rear exit. Its heavy steel door, equipped with a crash bar, was secure. Aside from the victim, he was alone in the store.

He returned to the counter, pulled on a pair of latex gloves, and knelt to check the victim for a pulse. He placed his fingers against Rizzoli's carotid artery and held them there. Nothing. He removed a mini mag flashlight from his duty belt and shined it into the victim's eyes. No pupillary response. Rizzoli was dead.

Weir glanced at the register. Its drawer was open.

As a symphony of sirens approached, he stood and radioed to the dispatcher once again.

"5 Charlie 7, code four. Victim is DOA. Requesting Squad on scene."

"Ten-four, 5 Charlie 7. Squad notified and en route."

Weir stepped outside to speak with any witnesses who had

stuck around. A crowd of pedestrians had gathered. When three additional cars pulled up, Weir tasked a backup officer named Newton with keeping onlookers away while he interviewed the breathless track-suited man who had flagged him down initially and an elderly gentleman holding a small barking dog.

"Which one of you went inside?" Weir asked.

"We both did," Breathless said, and the old man nodded in agreement.

Breathless turned out to be Maurice Graham, a retired dock worker who had stopped by Rizzi's to get his morning coffee and paper. He sported a pencil-thin mustache and gold-rimmed spectacles, and his track suit was out of style by several decades and at least two sizes too small for him. The tall old man with the dog was Leonard Hall. He wore a ratty wool overcoat over a rattier pair of jeans and a flannel shirt and smelled like a brewery. Hall introduced the dog as Happy, though the mutt's disposition implied otherwise.

"You both live around here?" Weir said.

"I'm just around the corner, off Mott," Graham said, gesturing with a thumb.

"What about you, Leonard?"

"Haven't got no home. I'm staying at the shelter near the Mission."

"What about Happy?" Newton said with a sneer. "They let her in the shelter, too?"

Happy vocalized her dissatisfaction, but Hall ignored the comment and went on scratching the dog's head.

"Did either of you see who did this?" Weir said.

"No," Graham said. "We literally walked in and found him dead."

"Did you touch anything?"

"No," Graham said. "I held the door on my way in for Mr.—"

"Leonard," Hall said. "Leonard Hall."

Weir detected a slight slur to Hall's speech. The old duffer had come to Rizzi's for a refill, he thought.

A half hour passed before the detectives arrived. By then, EMS had come, declared the victim officially dead—confirming Weir's earlier diagnosis—and gone.

Detective First Class McGovern waved Weir over to the front of the market, away from the witnesses.

This wasn't Weir's first encounter with McGovern. He'd had the unpleasant experience of dealing with the brusque know-it-all detective at other recent crime scenes. McGovern's most distinguishing feature was the ugly scar adorning his left cheek, though the huge chip on his shoulder ran a close second. Rumor had it the grizzled homicide dick had been a rookie himself when he'd chased an armed perp down an alleyway and was rewarded for his efforts when a bullet from the perp's gun grazed the side of his face.

"Okay, Rook, who are those two sorry bastards, and what did they have to say?" McGovern said.

"Witnesses. Maurice Graham and Leonard Hall."

"And what exactly did they witness?"

"Well, they didn't actually *witness* anything," Weir said. "They located the victim inside the bodega."

"You get statements yet?"

"Nothing written. I figured you'd want to speak to them."

McGovern lit a cigarette.

"I saw the cash drawer standing open," Weir said, attempting to be helpful. "I figure it's a robbery gone bad."

"Oh, is that what you figure, Officer Weir? Sounds like you got this thing wrapped up. Not sure why I'm even here."

Weir knew there was nothing he could say that would make McGovern back off, so he simply took it.

"Tell you what, Sherlock, why don't you send Mr. Track Suit over here?"

"Maurice Graham," Weir said.

"Whatever."

"What about Mr. Hall?"

McGovern pointed his nicotine-stained fingers at Hall. "That one's yours, Rook. By the looks of him, he probably smells worse than his mutt."

"Careful you don't get bit, kid," Newton teased, and McGovern laughed.

After sending Graham over to McGovern, Weir asked Hall to take a seat inside his squad car and lowered all the windows to keep the vagrant's body odor from overpowering him. "How long have you been staying at the shelter?" he asked.

"Couple weeks, I guess. I'm not from around here. Other than Happy, I don't have any friends."

"They don't allow pets at that shelter," Weir said, challenging him.

"I know. Truth is, they kicked me out about a week ago, when I tried to bring Happy inside."

As if in response to Hall's comment, Happy let out several ear-splitting yaps at something unseen.

"I've been living on the street since then," Hall continued. "Figured if I told you that, I might be in trouble."

"No law against being homeless," Weir said. "Tell me again why you happened to be in Rizzi's this morning."

"I took Happy for a walk. We ended up here because I needed a refill."

"Booze?"

Hall gave him a wry smile. "Like Jacob, I wrestle with the angel."

"Who's Jacob?"

"In the Bible? Book of Genesis?"

Weir nodded. "Then you went inside the bodega?"

"Yeah, like that guy in the running suit said—"

"Graham?"

"Yes, Mr. Graham. We went in and found the guy lying dead on the floor."

"And you're sure neither of you touched anything?"

Hall shook his head. "I didn't. I can't say about Mr. Graham. Soon as I saw the body, I beat feet outside."

"And there were no other customers inside, either before you two entered or after?"

"Not a one. I did see a junkie walking by, when I first approached the store. Happy didn't like him much. I don't know where he was coming from."

"Could he have been inside the store before you saw him?"

"I wouldn't hazard a guess. Maybe."

"Can you describe him? The junkie."

"Tall, pale, long stringy hair, insane eyes. Looked like he was with the fever."

"Fever?"

"Like he needed a fix."

"Clothing?"

"Can't give you details, but he wasn't dressed much better than me. Shabby was my first impression."

Weir looked up at the sound of a whistle. McGovern was waving him back to the scene. "Would you excuse me for a second, Mr. Hall?"

"Certainly, officer. Happy and I will wait right here."

"Well?" McGovern said. "Is your dog man the victim or the crime?"

"Excuse me?"

"Not a fan of the Dead, I guess. It's an old joke, Rook."

"Over my head. You sound like Hall."

"How's that?" McGovern said. He cocked his head to one side and withdrew another cigarette from his pack.

"He quotes scripture," Weir said.

"Did he give you anything useful?"

"Said he saw a junkie hurrying past as he neared the bodega, but nothing beyond that."

"Track Suit didn't mention a junkie."

"They might have come from different directions."

"Maybe. Or he's just jerkin' your chain, Weir. We'll canvass the neighborhood for surveillance cameras."

They turned toward the sound of a ruckus near the barricades.

One of the officers was challenging a man in a charcoal suit.

"That's got to be a Fed," McGovern said, dropping his cigarette on the sidewalk and crushing it under the sole of his black Oxford.

"How do you know?" Weir said.

"Trust me, kid. I've been at this a long time."

They approached the commotion, and the detective said, "What's up?"

"Marshal Dillon here doesn't seem to understand the word no," the uniformed cop said.

The man in the suit flashed his credentials.

"Marshal, huh?" McGovern said, inspecting the ID. "Slow day, Deputy Gerrit?"

"I need to speak to you in private," Gerrit said.

"I'm busy, Marshal. Little thing called murder."

"It's important."

McGovern rolled his eyes. "Always is. Okay, let 'im through." At the entrance to the bodega, McGovern stopped and said, "Okay, you got my attention. What's so important the Federales feel compelled to crash my scene?"

"Your victim named Rizzoli?"

McGovern glanced at Weir. "This guy, it's like he's psychic or something." His attention returned to Gerrit. "Yeah, Franklin Rizzoli. And he won't be coming down to breakfast, in case you were looking to speak with him. Mind telling me why you care?"

Gerrit looked around uneasily before answering. "Rizzoli's not his real name."

"Come again?" McGovern said.

"His real name is Louis Vincenzo, and he's been in WITSEC for the past ten years. May I ask how he died?"

"You seem to have all the answers, Gerrit. I'm surprised you don't already know. He was shot. Looks like a robbery. Why?"

"Mr. Vincenzo was one of two guys we relocated from another part of the country. They testified against a crime boss in return for new lives."

"Remind me never to testify against a crime boss," McGovern said, exhaling a plume of bluish smoke. "So how is it you just happen to show up right after someone turns this Vincenzo-Rizzoli guy into a corpse?"

"I didn't just show up. We've been monitoring Vincenzo since last month, when the other witness was gunned down in L.A."

"Nice work," McGovern said, as they watched the stretcher and body bag containing the victim being removed from the store. "Any idea who we should be looking for?"

"We think the mobster brought in a pro. Any chance you had witnesses?"

"Two, so far. Mr. Track Suit here"—McGovern pointed to a nervous looking Maurice Graham—"and a scripture-quoting street bum named—"

"—Leonard Hall," Weir said.

"Where's he?" Gerrit said.

"In my blue-and-white, with his dog."

The three of them turned to Weir's radio car and saw that it was unoccupied.

"I don't know how to tell you this, Rook," McGovern commented drily, "but it looks like your man might be a rank deceiver."

"He can't have gone far," Weir said hopefully. "Maybe he took the dog for a walk?"

"Wouldn't bet my paycheck on it," McGovern said.

"What did this dog walker look like?" Gerrit said.

"Tall, thin, ratty overcoat," Weir said.

"Don't forget the BO and the mangy mutt," McGovern said.

"How old was he?" Gerrit said.

"Not sure," Weir said. "Definitely an older guy, like close to sixty."

"Hey, easy with that older-guy crap, Junior," McGovern said through a plume of smoke.

Gerrit removed a black-and-white photograph from the inside breast pocket of his suit coat. "He look anything like this?"

The two cops studied the grainy image, which appeared to be an enlarged still from a surveillance video. The man depicted was much thinner than the vagrant calling himself Leonard Hall.

"Hell, I didn't get close enough to tell," McGovern said.

Weir's face blanched, and McGovern noticed.

"Is it him, or isn't it?" McGovern said.

"I guess it could be the same guy," Weir said at last. "But he—"

"Who is he?" McGovern said.

"We don't know his identity, but we think this may be the man the mobster hired to assassinate our witnesses."

"Nice going, kid," McGovern said to Weir. "I'll cut Track Suit loose. We better go find Hall."

Back in his rented hotel room, the man calling himself Maurice Graham went directly to the bathroom and turned on the shower. He peeled off his tracksuit and fake mustache and stuffed them into a trash bag. Standing in front of the mirror, he removed the silicone pregnancy prosthetic and turned it over to reveal the false bottom he had painstakingly hollowed out to accept the handgun and silencer he'd used to kill Louis Vincenzo.

As he removed the gun and tossed the prosthesis, he wondered how long it would take the cops to realize they had been duped. After killing the store's owner and hiding the gun in the phony belly, he had exited through the rear door of the bodega, then circled around to the front, as if entering for the first time. Experience had taught him there was nothing better than reporting your own crime to buy yourself time and cast suspicion elsewhere. The presence of the old wino to back his story had been a stroke of luck.

Graham grinned at his reflection in the mirror. Murder for hire was all about patience and self-control. And sometimes good fortune smiles on those who need it most.

Epilogue: Live Dead
Wembley Arena concert (October 30, 1990)

SET LIST

"Jack Straw"
"Bertha"
"Wang Dang Doodle"
"Brown Eyed Women"
"Queen Jane Approximately"
"Row Jimmy"
"Let It Grow"
"Valley Road"
"Picasso Moon"
"Foolish Heart"
"Looks Like Rain"
"Lady With a Fan"/"Terrapin Station"
"Drums"
"Space"
"The Wheel"
"I Need a Miracle"
"Black Peter"
"Turn On Your Love Light"
"The Weight"

LADY WITH A FAN
Avram Lavinsky

It had been a relatively slow night at Amethyst. The music and colored lights went off at four in the morning. The fluorescent lights came on. One bouncer unlocked the main entrance for the last of the stragglers, then locked up again behind them, while the other checked that the bathrooms were empty.

Her feet sore, her energy drained, Safia finished wiping down the last of the tables and flipping over the chairs for the cleaning crew.

Antoine was balancing the register, while behind him Chloé the barback scrubbed down the ice well and the metal speed rack.

"That investment banker, Lambert," said Antoine, looking over his shoulder at Safia. "He sure is into you. For a while there, he wouldn't take no for an answer."

On the other side of the bar, Delphine stared into her phone's calculator app, determining the splits on the pool of server tips. "Our cruel Safia, stealing half an old man's heart."

Antoine slipped a rubber band over a stack of bills. "Not sure he has much to steal. She could have taken half his wallet, though. He was up to eighteen hundred euros by the time I had him tossed."

"Business is business," said Delphine, frowning at her phone. "Love is love. She has a love date tonight."

"We finally get to meet the mysterious Tomi, then," said Antoine.

Delphine slid a small stack of bills toward Safia, mostly ones and fives.

Safia pocketed the money. "Never."

Delphine stared at the entrance. "Well, now. I can see why."

Masked by reflections, haloed by a streetlamp, Tomi's perfectly proportioned form filled the frame of the glass door.

Seeing him, Safia's spirits lifted, and a surge of energy erased her weariness. She trotted to the door and unlocked it.

Slipping out into the predawn air was like slipping into another universe. She flew to Tomi and placed her hands against his chest. His arms encircled her, and his laugh vibrated beneath her palms. She ached to kiss him but not with the others watching through the door. She took his hand and pulled him toward the Rue de Belleville and her apartment in Ménilmontant.

He asked her how work had been, and she surprised herself by her need to tell him about it. She said nothing of Lambert, the investment banker, but the bussers had been so slow and the businessmen so rude. She found herself cursing and gesturing wildly. Then, turning to Tomi, she saw nothing, only her own shadow. He'd vanished.

"Up here."

She looked up.

Tomi sat on one of the limbs of a branching streetlight, an ancient iron structure four meters high, with three hexagonal lamps that cast his fair skin in a tangerine hue. He kicked his legs as a toddler might in a chair sized for a grownup.

Like a trapeze artist, he stood, folded, and swung down, hanging for an instant, then dropping to the pavement in perfect balance.

She leaned a shoulder into him as they walked. "Where did you learn to climb like that?"

He placed an arm gently around her waist, and they ambled past shops with their security gates rolled down, the windows on their upper levels dark. "All kids climb, but I got serious about it right here in Père Lachaise."

"The cemetery?"

"When I was thirteen, we spent most of our time there. We started competitions, balancing on the tombstones, jumping from one stone to another."

"I think I know who won."

"Always. We turned the place into a parkour playground. We climbed statues. We did tricks on the roofs of the mausoleums. I used to land flips jumping from one burial vault to another."

"Didn't it bother you, knowing what was at your feet?"

"Not really. I didn't see it as disrespectful. Sometimes I'd read the epitaphs. There was one; it was in Italian, a painter, if I remember: *Morte lo colse quando giunse alla gloria.* 'Death overtook him when he came to glory.' I remember thinking, *Yeah, that's what it's about. That's all that matters. Taking your one chance to do one thing, something truly special.*"

Safia caressed his shoulder. "You think people do only one special thing in their whole lifetime?"

"The lucky ones. The rest never get a shot at all."

The hollow tone in his voice made her stop walking. Reaching up, she pulled him into a kiss, and when their lips parted, she looked into his gunmetal-gray eyes, a single point of light from a streetlamp shining in each. She could never live in his world of one all-consuming obsession. She felt the city around her, and everywhere she saw countless paths forward.

Though he researched the Musée d'Orsay for weeks, Tomi found himself transfixed by its scale and its singular grandeur when he finally paid the fourteen euros and entered the building. The interior resembled the central nave of a cathedral. Immense arches, rising to a height of five stories and decorated with hundreds of sculpted rosettes, formed the skeleton of its ceiling, connected by glass panels framed in wrought iron. Two arcades of smaller arches running the length of the structure formed the armature of the sidewalls, also connected by glass panels.

The building retained much of its identity as a railway station during the Belle Epoch. In fact, the departing Express Régional, which still ran beneath it, vibrated the floor as Tomi made his way to the first statues. He admired each in turn, stealing glances at the strategically placed black boxes—the motion detectors, their LED lights flickering from green to red as he passed.

On the mezzanine level, one motion detector didn't change. On the uppermost level, among the Impressionists, his excitement grew as he found another in the same state. With a surge of adrenaline, he noticed that two of the sensors remained unlit entirely.

When he finally came to Pissarro's *Portrait of the Artist*, he understood why De la Cour's buyer would want to obtain it by any means. The more abstract shapes in the background and the exaggerated lighting had an emotional truth, a certain perfect wholeness. With his long white beard and dark eyes, Pissarro seemed timeless and yet distinctly of his time, a myth personified.

Tomi rounded a corner and passed signs for a temporary exhibit. The dazzling colors of a square canvas captured his eye, a work by Klimt, a portrait of a woman in a dress of Oriental style, eyes alight, the glowing skin of one shoulder exposed above her fan. He was unable to look away.

Few cars cruised Place Henry-de-Montherlant after two in the morning. Tomi listened for other footsteps behind him but heard only the hum of the streetlamps and the waves of the Seine lapping against its embankments. He had his bag strapped over his shoulder, his gloved hands deep in the pockets of a heavy beige sweatshirt that matched the limestone façades of the buildings. At the old Caisse des Dépôts building, he scrambled up the grated window and swung over the stone balustrade onto the terrace. Confident he had not been seen, he began to scale the building. The decorative sills and cornices made for easy climbing. He reached the roof in seconds and crossed it.

The west face of the Musée d'Orsay rose above him, and beyond that the glass-and-iron terminus of the central chamber. A single security camera on the roof of the museum had a view of his path. He'd disabled it on a previous visit with a mixture of white glue and earth that mimicked bird droppings.

He made his way around the tower and started up the arched roof of the chamber. Near the apex, he removed the glass cutter from his shoulder bag and set to work, scoring the widest section he could manage. When he was satisfied with the depth of the cut, he fastened a suction cup and, with a few sharp yanks, pulled the oval of glass from the pane.

He took out a length of climbing rope and secured it to the stone ornament at the roof's peak. He would need this for his return trip. Dangling from the ornament, he swung himself through the new opening.

His boots came down on an iron grating, and he found himself in a forest of metal above the museum's glass ceiling. Here the wrought-iron ribs of the supporting arches were unadorned, and countless smaller beams and struts supported the roof. The lighting from the central chamber below gave the space a spectral feeling. Walkways traced the uppermost perimeter of the structure for maintenance access. He expected no motion sensors and found none. Descending a metal stairway and coming to a door to the upper level, he was about to take out his lock picks, but there was no keyhole, only a thumb turn. With a shake of his head, he unlocked it and stepped through.

He found Pissarro's self-portrait, took it down and leaned it back-side-out against the wall. He took a screwdriver from his bag and removed the backing structure from the frame, but he couldn't risk taking the time to remove the ancient tacks from the canvas. He drew out his razor and cut the canvas where it wrapped around the stretcher, careful to sacrifice no more of it than necessary.

Here he should have removed the stretcher from the frame,

separated the canvas, and carefully placed it, with the painting facing out, in the compartment between the layers of his sweatshirt, which was really two sweatshirts sewn together for this very purpose. He didn't.

He went to the adjacent wall, to Klimt's *Lady with a Fan.*

"What have you done?" Jean-Raphaël De la Cour stared down into the boot of Tomi's Peugeot 308, looking as if he might vomit. Even through the layer of white tissue paper above it, he could recognize the outline of Camille Pissarro's bearded face. It was the layers of paper and canvas beneath it that alarmed him.

"I did what you hired me to do." Tomi's voice echoed in the bottom level of the parking garage, empty except for the two men and their vehicles. He flipped over the layer of tissue paper as if opening a book. The Pissarro leaped to life, the painter's dark eyes peering out across a century.

"You crazy bastard! I told you the Pissarro. Just the Pissarro." De la Cour pulled a handkerchief from his pocket and patted his brow. "Every news agency in every major city in the world is running the story. They'll set up a task force. They'll come for us with sirens blaring. Why would you be so foolhardy?"

"Half the alarms at the Musée d'Orsay weren't functioning. It was the one and only chance. They won't let it happen again. And I won't hand you a thirty-million-euro painting for ninety thousand again, either."

"Thirty million at Sotheby's, maybe." De la Cour's tone grew shrill. "The Saudi wouldn't budge from a hundred and eighty thousand. He's taking a big risk, too, you know."

Tomi guessed that the old man had set up the deal for closer to eight hundred thousand, but he didn't press the point. He'd agreed to do the job for ninety thousand.

Tentatively, De la Cour reached down to flip over the canvas.

Tomi's hand shot out and grabbed his wrist. "Of course, unless you're taking the other paintings on consignment, you don't need to see them, right?"

Locked in the younger man's granite grip, De la Cour sensed danger with an immediacy he had not appreciated before. "Yes. Consignment. Yes, of course."

The hand released him, and De la Cour carefully flipped the Pissarro facedown onto the tissue paper. Then he turned over the sheet beneath it.

Vincent Cormier's *Madame Bochcova*, styled after the work of Klimt.

Jeune Fille au Jardin by Mary Cassatt, her broad brushstrokes emblematic of Impressionism, but the figure in the foreground rendered more traditionally.

Claude Monet's *The Poppy Field*, the mother and child drifting spirit-like through hills dotted with orange flowers.

Feeling a film of cold sweat sheeting over him, he flipped the Monet over and gasped at the sight of the last painting. *Lady With a Fan* was Klimt's final work, some said his greatest. The elegant and graceful contours of the woman's face in three-quarter view, a few tight ringlets of hair drifting into her face, one shoulder bare. The vibrant colors of the fan against her floral dress, the dazzling background of lotus flowers and exotic birds. No one could forecast its value at auction. Klimt's *Portrait of Adele Bloch-Bauer* had sold for a hundred and thirty-five million in 2006, the highest figure ever paid for a painting at the time.

The two men stared at the work in silence. The painting's molten colors swirled in Tomi's eyes. How could De la Cour question his decision to take it? There had been no decision. There was no universe in which he did not take it. He had always taken it, and he always would take it. He had been born to steal it, just as Klimt had been born to paint it.

Safia woke suddenly. The glowing crimson numbers of her alarm clock showed it was three in the morning. She'd grown accustomed to the nearby rumble of the Paris Metro, but unexpected sounds could still rouse her.

A faint creak made her sit up and pull the sheet over her bare shoulders.

Something filled the shadowy space of her narrow bedroom doorway.

"Tomi?"

"Yes, it's me." He had a sweatshirt over his arm. He placed it across the back of a chair.

Then he came to her and knelt at her bedside.

She ran her hands over the rounded muscles of his shoulders, his T-shirt only slightly damp with sweat, the strap of his shoulder bag rough beneath her fingers. She pulled his head against her breast. "God! You scared me. You don't have to do that. Call me. Knock."

"I didn't want to wake you."

"Well, I'm awake now." She stroked his hair. He'd buzzed it short. It grazed the sides of her fingers, soft and fine as a baby's. She kissed his forehead.

As he started to rise, she wrapped her arms and legs around him. He lifted her and turned, pinning her naked back against the wall. She brought her open mouth against his lips and kissed him hard. He wriggled, and his shoulder bag dropped loudly to the floorboards.

"You brought your rock collection with you?"

"Just a bag full of money."

They made love urgently, frantically, changing positions at random intervals, desperate to unleash withheld passion.

Later, she lay with her ear against his chest, listening to the steady thump of his heart. She knew what he was thinking. She rested her chin on her hands and looked up at him. "Go on. Say it. I know you want to."

"I have no right to."

She had never seen eyes so gray. Even with his lids half

closed, they worked a strange magic on her, or maybe they just reflected the strange magic that existed between them. "You always have a right to tell me your feelings."

His lips drew together as he found the words. "I don't want to share you. I don't want you to sell yourself."

"Everybody sells a little of themself."

"It's not jealousy. I don't care that you work at the club. But the escort stuff...it's just...there's nothing in it for you. Nothing except danger and debasement."

"And six hundred euros a night. I don't want to, either, but I have to live. It's only a couple of times a week. I could do it more, but I don't."

Tomi looked into her eyes again. "I hate thinking about what you do with those men."

"You'd be surprised how many of them don't want me to do anything...other than hang on their arm at a party or sit across from them at dinner. It's pathetic, really."

"But the others."

"I have my rules."

"How do you know they aren't fresh out of a lunatic asylum?"

She traced his collarbone with one finger. His skin was many shades fairer than her own but weathered. If she didn't know he was twenty-nine, six years older than her, she might mistake him for thirty-five or forty, despite his enormous chest and chiseled muscles. "The cover charge at Amethyst is a little steep for a guy in that situation."

"Do you want to do it forever?"

"If I did, why would I be taking courses at university?"

His expression hardened. "People always think that way. Then they end up doing that same one thing their entire lives."

Their second time was far more patient. It left Safia utterly drained and a little sore. Moments after they climaxed, she felt herself drifting into a deep sleep.

Tomi lay on his side and listened until her breathing grew regular, then he slipped out of the bed. He brought his shoulder bag into the tiny kitchen and unzipped it, feeling his way past the glass cutting tools to remove the duct tape and the nine banded stacks of bills.

The woman outside Safia Abadi's fifth-floor apartment identified herself as Anne-Claire Brissard of the Police Nationale, Brigade de Répression du Banditisme. She wore a navy-blue blazer over a simple white blouse, black jeans—and no Gendarmerie armband.

"I'm afraid it's not a good time," Safia said. "I was just about to mop." This was mostly true. In fact, she had been just about to mop twenty minutes ago when she flipped the two chairs onto the tiny table in her kitchenette and was distracted by the nine bundles of hundred-euro notes neatly duct-taped to the bottom of one of them.

"Please, I'll only need a few moments of your time."

Safia snuck a look back at the chairs, convincing herself that the bundles were hidden from view, then looked up into the taller woman's face, more handsome than pretty and made up with only merlot-red lipstick and a hint of eyeliner. "All right. I guess so." She swung the door open and stepped back enough to let Madame Brissard enter.

"May we sit?"

"Of course. Can I get you anything?" Hopefully the woman understood that "anything" meant water or coffee without milk.

Brissard raised her palm. "I'm fine."

Safia backed into the living room, hoping Brissard would follow. "So...what brings you here?"

"I'm looking for Tomislav Zagorac."

"Is he in trouble?"

"We need to clear him of involvement in something. I'm investigating a crime that resembles one he was a suspect in two years ago. Do you know where I can find Monsieur Zagorac?"

"I don't. Honestly." This was also true. "He comes and goes. Sometimes for weeks at a time, and he never keeps a phone number for very long."

"And the last time you saw him?"

"I—I'm not sure. I guess...it's been a while. He was here in April, I remember."

"You don't have any contact information for his family? Maybe a friend?"

"Sorry. I can't help you there."

Brissard's stony expression and the weighty silence between her questions convinced Safia that she knew everything. The woman could scent her fear. She could see the sheen of sweat on her forehead and hear the pounding of her pulse.

Then, miraculously, Brissard drifted towards the door. She handed Safia a business card and asked her to phone immediately if she heard from Tomi.

Safia bolted the door and leaned into it, closing her eyes, as Brissard's footsteps on the stairway faded into silence.

She heard nothing from Tomi for eight days. Then, on a Monday evening, clothed in her bathrobe and flip flops, a sudden motion in her living-room window surprised her.

Tomi swung his legs over the radiator, ducking his head under the yellow valance. Somewhere below, a car honked angrily. Tomi slid the window shut, muffling a longer honk. His raised eyebrows seemed to signal a warning to keep silent.

She kept her voice low. "What are you doing?"

He crossed to her kitchen and motioned her to follow.

He reached behind the refrigerator and removed a large white square. Laying it on the table, he removed a covering of tissue paper to reveal a painting, a portrait of a woman holding a fan across her chest. She had the slender form of a dancer, the tapered corners of her lips slightly upturned in a hint of a mischievous grin, her floral dress draped low on one arm.

"On the news," said Safia, "they keep saying *five* paintings were taken."

"I left four with a dealer I know."

"Why not this one, too?"

"I wanted to. I just couldn't. She spoke to me...really...I *heard* her voice. She said she wouldn't forgive me if I gave her to him. Now they've arrested him, and I'm afraid he may have destroyed the other four."

"Destroyed them?"

"To get rid of the evidence. He told me what he would do if they closed in on him. Burn the stolen art and put the ashes down the garbage disposal."

"So then all of it...for nothing?"

"For ninety thousand euros...and a moment of triumph."

"I found the money. Someone came here from the Police Nationale. She could have found it. She could have arrested me."

"I know." He looked down. "I'm sorry."

"And if they've arrested that dealer, won't they come for you?"

"They will. I'm going to lie low in the south for a while. You could come with me."

She felt a jolt at the prospect but struggled to tamp down her excitement. She needed to be sure. They both did. "Wouldn't we be safer apart?"

He fidgeted, his giant hands clasped, his eyes timid. "We could give it at least a try."

She leapt at him, wrapping her arms around his neck, rising on her toes to cover his face in kisses.

Twenty minutes later, in the passenger seat of his Peugeot, she read the phone number from the business card and tapped it into her phone.

"Brissard."

"*Bonjour*, Madame Brissard. It's Safia, Safia Abadi."

"*Bonjour*. You have something for me?"

"I know where the last painting is."

"You know the location of one of the paintings stolen from the

Musée d'Orsay?"

"Yes."

"Tell me about it." Brissard sounded slightly skeptical.

"It's the one by Klimt." She looked at Tomi for confirmation. He nodded. "*Lady with a Fan.*"

"It's not destroyed?" Brissard's voice ratcheted up in pitch, her words coming in a torrent. "And you know where it is?"

"Yes. And no, it's not destroyed at all. It's in my apartment."

"Why are you coming forward now? Why not when I questioned you before?"

"I just learned about it."

"From Tomislav Zagorac?"

Safia looked at Tomi, his eye behind his sunglasses focused on the road ahead. She said nothing.

"Can you tell me where he is?"

"No. I have to go."

"No! Stay on the line. You realize there is a sizeable reward in place."

"Go get the painting, please. She's waiting."

"Think about it. You might be in line for a half a million if you can lead us to him."

She tapped the red disconnect button on her screen. She would not be bought or sold, not any longer. She was *late*, and she knew, in the way a woman knows, that she carried Tomi's child. Perhaps Tomi had completed his singular act of glory. Perhaps he would pay the price. She would complete many smaller acts of glory. She would become many things. In the way every mother had since the dawn of time.

ACKNOWLEDGMENTS

My thanks to the authors who enthusiastically contributed stories, to Eric Campbell and Lance Wright at Down & Out Books for greenlighting my seventh "inspired by" anthology, to my wife Laurie Pachter and daughter Rebecca Jones as always and for always...and, most of all, to Jerry Garcia and the Dead. What a long, strange trip it's been!

ABOUT THE CONTRIBUTORS

DAVID AVALLONE is a writer, filmmaker, and host of the award-winning podcast *The Writers Block*. His writing credits include *Batwheels* (Warner Brothers Animation) and several comic-book series, including *Elvira Meets H.P. Lovecraft* (Dynamite) and *Drawing Blood* (Image). He's also written such iconic characters as Zorro, Vampirella, Red Sonja, The Shadow, Doc Savage, John Carter/Dejah Thoris, Kolchak, Bettie Page, and Nick Carter, and he's worked on both the *Star Wars* and *Planet of the Apes* franchises. The son of prolific novelist Michael Avallone and women's rights activist Fran Avallone, he lives in Hollywood with his delightful wife Augusta and three mischievous cats. *DavidAvalloneFreelance.com*

DOMINIQUE BIEBAU is a Belgian author. His second thriller, *Russian for Beginners,* won both the Hercule Poirot Prize and the Golden Noose, the two most important awards for Dutch-language crime fiction; a short-story version of the novel appeared in *Ellery Queen's Mystery Magazine* and was a finalist for the International Thriller Writers' Best Short Story award. His sixth book, *The Christie Murders*, was published in April 2024. When he's not writing, he teaches Dutch in a secondary school and lives with his wife and two children in the vicinity of Brussels.

PAUL AWAD is an author, filmmaker, screenwriter, and cinema professor. His debut novel, *When Earth Shall Be No More*, co-

written with Kathryn O'Sullivan, won the 2023 IPPY Bronze Medal Award in Science Fiction. Though he has written numerous screenplays, "Touch of Grey" is his first published short story. His award-winning film work includes the documentary *Bicentennial Bonsai: Emissaries of Peace*, the crime feature *A Savage Nature*, and the Western series *Thurston*.
Paul-Awad.com

BRUCE ROBERT COFFIN is a retired detective sergeant, the author of the Detective Byron mysteries and the forthcoming Detective Justice mysteries, and the co-author (with LynDee Walker) of the Turner and Mosley Files series. He has won Killer Nashville's Silver Falchion for Best Procedural and Best Investigator and the Maine Literary Award for Best Crime Fiction, and he's been a finalist for the Agatha Award for Best Contemporary Novel and the Anthony Award for Best Short Story.
BruceRobertCoffin.com

JAMES D.F. HANNAH is the Shamus Award-winning author of the Henry Malone series, including the novels *Behind the Wall of Sleep* and *Because the Night*. His short fiction has appeared in EQMM, *Vautrin*, *Rock and a Hard Place*, and *Shotgun Honey*, and in anthologies including *Eight Very Bad Nights*, *Playing Games*, *Under the Thumb*, *Only the Good Die Young,* and *Best American Mystery and Suspense 2022*. He lives in Louisville, Kentucky, where all the bourbon is.
JamesDFHannah.com

VINNIE HANSEN is a Claymore and Silver Falchion finalist and the author of the Carol Sabala mystery series, the novels *Lostart Street* and *One Gun*, and more than sixty short stories. *Crime Writer*, a suspense novel companion to *One Gun*, is due from Level Best Books in the summer of 2025. Still sane(ish) after twenty-seven years of teaching high-school English, she has retired and plays keyboards with ukulele groups in Santa Cruz,

California, where she lives with her husband and the requisite cat.
VinnieHansen.com

JAMES L'ETOILE uses his twenty-nine years behind bars as an influence in his award-winning novels, short stories, and screenplays. He is a former associate warden in a maximum-security prison, hostage negotiator, and director of California's state parole system. His novels have been shortlisted or awarded the Lefty, Anthony, Silver Falchion, and Public Safety Writers awards. *Face of Greed* and *Served Cold* are his most recent novels. Look for *River of Lies*, coming soon.
JamesLetoile.com

LINDA LANDRIGAN has been the editor-in-chief of *Alfred Hitchcock's Mystery Magazine* since 2002. She edited the commemorative anthology *Alfred Hitchcock's Mystery Magazine Presents Fifty Years of Crime and Suspense* (2006) and the e-anthology *Alfred Hitchcock's Mystery Magazine Presents Thirteen Tales of New American Gothic* (2012). In 2019, she received the Ellery Queen Award from the Mystery Writers of America for her service to the mystery-publishing industry. She graduated from New College in Sarasota (FL) and received her master's from Dartmouth College in Hanover (NH).

AVRAM LAVINSKY is a recovering musician with one gold record and countless unsold ones in his attic. His prose has been shortlisted for the Al Blanchard Award for New England's best crime story, the Claymore for best YA novel, and the Brooklyn Non-Fiction Prize. His recent publishing credits include *Mystery Tribune, Shotgun Honey, Punk Noir, Black Cat Weekly, Deadly Nightshade: Best New England Crime Stories 2022*, and *The Best Mystery Stories of the Year 2023*.
AvramLavinsky.com

G.M. MALLIET writes mystery novels and cozies. She is best known for *Death of a Cozy Writer,* which won an Agatha Award, was named among the best books of 2008 by *Kirkus Reviews,* and was the first installment of her St. Just series. The holder of degrees from Oxford University and the University of Cambridge, she wrote for national and international news publications (Thomson Reuters) and public broadcasters (PBS) before making the switch to fiction writing.
GMMalliet.com

K.L. MURPHY is the author of *Her Sister's Death* (a 2023 Silver Falchion finalist for Best Mystery and a Once Upon a Book Club pick), the Detective Cancini series (*A Guilty Mind, Stay of Execution,* and *The Last Sin*), *Last Girl Missing* (the first book in a new series), and several short stories.
KellieLarsenMurphy.com

KATHRYN O'SULLIVAN is a Malice Domestic Best First Traditional Mystery Novel winner and author of the Colleen McCabe series. Her latest novel, *When Earth Shall Be No More,* co-written with Paul Awad, won the 2023 IPPY Bronze Medal in Science Fiction. Her short stories and ten-minute plays have been published in several anthologies, and her films include *Bicentennial Bonsai: Emissaries of Peace,* the crime feature *A Savage Nature,* and the Western series *Thurston.*
KathrynOsullivan.com

JOSH PACHTER was the 2020 recipient of the Short Mystery Fiction Society's Golden Derringer for Lifetime Achievement. His stories appear in EQMM, AHMM, and elsewhere, and he is the author of the novels *Dutch Threat* and *First Week Free at the Roomy Toilet.* He edits anthologies (including Anthony Award finalists *The Beat of Black Wings: Crime Fiction Inspired by the Songs of Joni Mitchell, Paranoia Blues: Crime Fiction Inspired by the Songs of Paul Simon,* and *Happiness Is a Warm Gun: Crime*

Fiction Inspired by the Songs of the Beatles) and translates fiction and nonfiction from multiple languages—mostly Dutch—into English.
JoshPachter.com

TWIST PHELAN is the author of the Finn Teller Corporate Spy and Pinnacle Peak mystery series, the stand-alone mystery *The Target*, and the middle-grade mystery *Snowed*. Her novels have been praised by *Publishers Weekly*, *Library Journal*, *Kirkus*, and *Booklist*. She also writes short stories, which have been published in EQMM and several Mystery Writers of America anthologies. Accolades for her work include two Thriller Awards, the Arthur Ellis Award, and nominations for the Shamus, Anthony, Derringer, Crime Writers of Canada Award of Excellence, and Irish Book awards.
TwistPhelan.com

FAYE SNOWDEN is the award-winning author of the southern gothic *Killing* series (Flame Tree Press), featuring homicide detective Raven Burns. Two of her short stories have been anthologized in *The Best American Mystery and Suspense* series (2021 and 2023 editions). She lives and writes from her home in Northern California.
FayeSnowden.com

JOSEPH S. WALKER lives in Indiana and teaches college literature and composition courses. His short fiction has appeared in AHMM, EQMM, *Mystery Weekly*, *Guilty*, *Tough*, *Mystery Tribune*, and a number of other magazines and anthologies, including three consecutive volumes of *The Mysterious Bookshop Presents the Best Mystery Stories of the Year*. He has been nominated for the Edgar and Derringer awards and has won the Bill Crider Prize for Short Fiction and the Al Blanchard Award (twice, in 2019 and 2021).
JSWalkerAuthor.com

On the following pages are a few
more great titles from the
Down & Out Books publishing family.

For a complete list of books and to
sign up for our newsletter,
go to DownAndOutBooks.com.

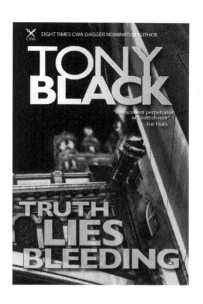

Truth Lies Bleeding
A DI Rob Brennan Case
Tony Black

Down & Out Books
August 2024
978-1-64396-384-6

Four teenagers find the mutilated corpse of a young girl stuffed into a dumpster in an Edinburgh alleyway. Who is she? Where did she come from? Who killed her and why? Above all, where is the baby to which she has obviously recently given birth?

Inspector Rob Brennan, recently back from psychiatric leave, is still shocked by the senseless shooting of his only brother. His superiors think that the case of the dumpster girl will be perfect to get him back on track. But Rob Brennan has enemies within the force, stacks of unfinished business and a nose for trouble. What he discovers about the murdered girl blows the case—and his life—wide open.

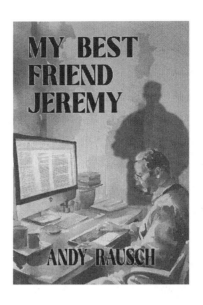

My Best Friend Jeremy
Andy Rausch

Down & Out Books
September 2024
978-1-64396-373-0

Chris is an indie horror author. He's not famous, and he's far from rich. He's just an everyday guy who works a day job. He's juggling a wife, kids, a mistress, and a day job, all while trying to find time to write his books. Since he's not broken through and had a major success, he's starting to doubt himself and question whether he should even continue writing.

When he starts receiving fan letters from a would-be writer named Jeremy, his passion for writing is rekindled. But after a couple of interactions go badly, Jeremy sets out to destroy Chris' life and career, and Chris realizes that nothing is off limits for his new fan. Are the people closest to Chris safe? Should he be concerned for his own life?

Tales of Music, Murder and Mayhem
Bouchercon Anthology 2024
Heather Graham, Editor

Down & Out Books
August 2024
978-1-64396-379-2

Indulge in twenty-four mesmerizing tales crafted by talented Bouchercon writers of mystery. These stories share a melody of music, murder, and mayhem: A gift given with strings attached, even to a cello, can backfire. Would you kill for that lucky break—kill to be the One? Do you recognize the murderous details hidden in that ballad's lyrics? When music and murder mix, will the past remain the past? Are the voices of the dead harmonizing in that hauntingly beautiful song? And more: stories of tailor-made revenge, the price of heckling, and the perils of being in a boy band.

New York State of Crime
Murder New York Style 6
Edited by D.M. Barr and Joseph R.G. De Marco,
with an Introduction by S.J. Rozan

Down & Out Books
September 2024
978-1-64396-376-1

New York is truly a state of crime. Nowhere is this better exempli-
fied than in this anthology, authored by acclaimed Sisters in Crime
NY/Tri-State authors Nancy Bilyeau, Susan Breen, Paula Bernstein,
D.M. Barr, Joseph R.G. De Marco, Susan Egan, Nancy Good, Nikki
Knight, Nina Mansfield, Adam Meyer, Karen Odden, Rebecca
Olmstead, Ellen Quint, Michelle Bazan Reed, Lori Robbins,
Catherine Siemann, Triss Stein, Cathi Stoler, Izolda Trakhtenberg,
and Nina Wachsman. On every page, these authors have created
tales of New Yorkers who take on unspeakable challenges. Your
challenge will be to stop reading before night turns to day.

Made in the USA
Columbia, SC
05 January 2025